Read about Bahar's gripping and redemptive past in this FREE, award-semi-finalist story.

For the latest book news, sign up at amyearls.com/behind-walls/.

PRAISE FOR UNDER HIS WINGS SERIES

Amy Earls crafts tales that are epic and unexpected, carefully weaving both faith and fantasy into narratives that are sure to thrill teen readers!

— LAUREN H. BRANDENBURG, MULTI-AWARD WINNING AUTHOR OF *THE DEATH OF MUNGO BLACKWELL*

The skill of a Christian author shines through when they are able to convey a message through character action, emotion, and exceptionally well-implemented symbolism instead of outright telling us. Lately, I've only found the heavy-handed latter, but Earls changed that streak, and I'm blissfully happy for it.

— ASHER SYED, READERS' FAVORITE 5-STAR REVIEW

A story to savor and an author to watch!

— TARA JOHNSON, AUTHOR OF *ALL THROUGH THE NIGHT*

Amy Earls delivers again with *Forbidden Reign*, a non-stop adventure leavened with humor and grace. Teen protagonist, Pero, strives to fulfill her divine calling, but discovers way more than she bargained for in a twist-filled ending. Perfect for fans of Christian speculative fiction!

— KAREN GRUNST, YA AUTHOR OF THE SACRED FIRE SAGA

Amy Earls' *Forbidden Reign* is laced with friendship, forgiveness, and faith as teen girl Pero faces challenges that often seem too large to conquer. I am surprised and amused by Amy's perspective.

— HEIDI GAUL, AUTHOR

Amy Earls has done it again. She weaves Biblical principles into an enticing story of love and belonging.

— KANDI J. WYATT, YA AUTHOR OF DRAGON COURAGE SERIES

Quirky humor mixed with emotions and tension made *Forbidden Reign* a fun read.

— ESTRADA PUBLISHING REVIEW

FORBIDDEN REIGN

UNDER HIS WINGS
BOOK 2

AMY EARLS

This is a work of fiction. All of the characters, organizations, publications, and events portrayed in this novel are either products of the author's imagination or are used fictitiously.

ISBN 979-8-9874017-7-4 (hardback)
ISBN 979-8-9874017-4-3 (paperback)
ISBN 979-8-9874017-3-6 (ebook)

Cover design by Seventhstar Art, www.SeventhStarArt.com

Find out more at www.AmyEarls.com

BOOKS BY AMY EARLS

UNDER HIS WINGS

Behind Walls (Prequel)

The King's Feather (Book #1)

Forbidden Reign (Book #2)

*For my students, who reached out their hands as a bus drove me away from the high school in Shanghai.
I tattooed your cries on my heart.*

"I was afraid of the army, and I listened to them instead.
Please forgive me."

—King Saul

"Home isn't where you're from, it's where you find light
when all grows dark."

—Pierce Brown

1

恐惧

A fall doesn't last forever. Yet as my hand clutched air and a scream lodged in my throat, I wondered. How hard would I crash?

I smacked against a body. At least it felt like a body. The crunch of bones, the bend of flesh. I searched my way through the dark and found what felt like a finger. Cold and still.

With a scream that would've woken the dead, I scuttled away, my palms pressing into carpet, as I collided into another body. A grunt sounded, and I leapt back.

"Watch where you're going, Pero."

I found Carper's arm and hugged it. "I think I killed someone."

"Don't be so dramatic," Carper's voice said. "You only landed on yourself. You left a dead version of yourself in this universe, and now you're returning."

"That makes no sense."

"Has anything you've been through in the last month made sense?"

"Fair point."

When we left Earth a month earlier, the last I remembered

was being drugged, thrown into a limo, and waking up in the older universe, Origo. Now that I'd returned to Earth, had I restored to my old self? My soul felt lighter, as if I'd transported back as a different Pero Ruth Moshe: brave, fearless, a chosen girl full of faith.

Carper wiggled his arm from under my squeeze. "Where's the light?"

A quick pressure and pain dug into my foot. "Ouch. Be careful."

He stepped off.

"You could apologize." I reached my hands forward and met what felt like empty clothes, then hangers.

"Why would I do that?" I heard Carper's feet shuffling.

"Right. Because you apologizing a million times while we walked through the debris of Moon City wasn't enough. *I'm sorry. I'm sorry.*"

"I never said that."

"Ha!" Past the hanging clothes, I touched a wall, then bumped against something light but solid with my feet. Were those shoes? "And I suppose you don't remember crying your eyes out either."

"I definitely did not do that."

As much as Carper had changed for the better in the last week, his moodiness still exposed its annoying head. Or was that just his personality?

"Sometimes I wonder."

I heard Carper's hand meet the wall and brush against it. "About what?"

"If you're really a kid trapped inside a sixty-year-old's body."

"Watch it. I'm only fifty-six. And there are far too many stilettos in here."

"Say what?"

A light shone. I turned my head and blinked. A large closet held coats, dresses, and an impressive supply of heels.

"Oh, yeah," Carper said. "I forgot about him."

I turned to where he gazed behind me and gasped.

Jimmy lay unmoving on the floor. Carper had said Jimmy's body was left here on Earth when he was transported to Origo.

"Maybe you landed on Jimmy."

"Not myself?"

Carper shrugged. "Jimmy's body died here too while he was in Origo. But he's not returning."

"It feels so final now," I whispered. "You know, Jimmy helped me survive a lot, including you."

"Don't forget he also tried to kill us."

I recalled Jimmy in Moon City's mansion, a knife in his hand as he charged over to Carper. Somehow, we'd survived. "He wouldn't have killed me."

Carper raised a brow.

Without Jimmy, would I have come back? Would Carper have come with me, humbled?

Carper's lips tightened. "It should've been me." He didn't take his eyes off Jimmy.

"Perhaps. I mean, you *are* a murderer."

"I suppose I am."

I shrugged. "Should've been me, too."

Carper pivoted.

"Mom, Sam, and..." I swallowed. "...Henry are missing because of me."

"Doesn't mean you should've died."

I shook my head. "You don't know who I was before you found me. I was scared all the time. I can't trust that kind of heart. I'm not sure if it ever really beat at all."

"Getting effusive, are we?"

I smiled. "That's a big word for you."

"You underestimate me." Carper held his hand out to display the door ahead. "Shall we?"

"What about Jimmy?"

"We'll bury him later." Carper cleared his throat. "I'd like to take him to his homeland. I think he lived somewhere in the States."

"He's from a farm. In Green Meadow, actually."

Before he died, Jimmy gave the farm to Sam, which would've made it my property too if I had accepted Sam's offer to marry him. I shivered. *Marriage* was a big word. Would I marry Henry? We were kind of an item now. But was marriage always the right answer when you loved someone?

"Hello?" Carper waved a hand in front of my face.

I blinked. "Did you say something?"

Carper grinned. "I asked how you knew that Jimmy was from Green Meadow, while you were day dreaming."

I put my hands to my hot face. "Uh, Jimmy told me before he died." I tripped over a shoe on my way to the closet door. "Where are we, anyway?"

"When Jimmy and I kidnapped you, this is where we took you. We didn't want you knowing, just in case you escaped. You'd passed out, so we didn't need to worry about that. A portal into the other world usually opens in this closet. Don't know what's special about this place. Maybe it's built out of magical wood or something."

"You said Mom would be in China. Are we in China?"

"No. The Oregon coast, the nearest portal from where you lived in Green Meadow."

"We're near Dad! I need to see him!"

"We can try." Carper pushed the door open.

Outside the closet was a large and well-furnished bedroom with a huge vanity where sat a middle-aged woman in a black-laced dress, aiming a curling iron toward us.

"Cherry?" Carper asked.

The woman's curling iron and voice dropped. "Calvin."

"Who's Cherry?"

Carper took a step back. "What are you doing here?"

The woman named Cherry stayed frozen. "I should be asking you the same thing. You're supposed to be dead."

"You say that as if you wish I was."

"What am I supposed to say?" Cherry's voice shook, then strengthened, like she wasn't sure if she held back a couple of tear drops or a torrent.

"You called me by my first name," Carper said.

Cherry's eyes narrowed. "I wasn't about to jump into your arms and call you *Daddy*."

Wait. Carper had a daughter? I took in the same dark eyes, round face, and skin tone. The woman had to be Carper's daughter, whether she wanted to be or not.

Carper's eyes sparked with what looked like pain for a moment before turning unreadable once again. "Your English has improved."

No wonder Cherry seemed to have issues with her father. He was terrible at small talk.

"Why'd you come back?" Cherry's chest heaved, her gaze like a laser trained on her target.

He remained standing, seemingly stung with every word she cast his way. Could words cripple a man?

Carper stepped forward. "I know you don't want to see me."

Cherry smirked.

"I don't blame you. I was a terrible father. I caused...you're in pain because of me. But I want you to know that things are different. You won't believe me yet, but I'll prove it to you."

"How?"

"The fact that you're in Rose's spare room, in a party dress, tells me that you're working for Rose and he's throwing another celebration to cover up his latest con."

Cherry's mouth gaped as if she'd just been caught stealing. Was this the same Rose who'd taken Mom, Henry, and Sam? The room seemed to shrink, like Moon City's walls, moving in, so tight, so confining. I needed to get out of here.

Carper kept his direction solely on his daughter. "Rose might've told me you were here, but I didn't believe it. I also happen to know that Rose's plan involves Pero here and that he won't be pulling me in this time. He knows I've changed, gone to the other side. However you want to say it. Rose took her family and is after her blood as a fulfillment to the prophecy, just as I used to be."

Cherry looked at me as if she'd only then noticed someone else in the room.

"Pero is one of the three chosen and the daughter of your old friend, Bahar."

"Bahar's alive?" Cherry clutched the edge of the vanity.

"As long as Rose doesn't hurt her. I'm making things right this time, and the first thing I need to do is get this fifteen-year-old girl to her mom."

Cherry's gaze lingered on my face, then scanned my clothes that were caked in dust from Moon City's crumbled walls.

"Hi." I waved. "I'm Pero, and I'm seventeen, not fifteen. Just so we're clear. You were friends with my mom?"

Cherry's lips curved into a slight smile. "You don't look anything like her. Maybe her nose."

Now was not the time to explain my adoption. I'd waited seventeen years to find out myself. Besides, Mom was still very much Mom, no matter the circumstance.

Carper clapped his hands. "Great. Since introductions have been made and we're all aware that Bahar and I are not dead, I will let you two get ready for the party." He bowed his head. "I trust Pero is in good hands." Carper turned and stepped up to a door leading out of the room.

What was he doing? He couldn't leave me there. Even as Carper's daughter, Cherry obviously wasn't on our side. Panic grew until I felt it might burst into a million pieces of tangible fear. What did fear look like, anyway? Crumbled rocks? Splintered wood? This wasn't the time to play another one of Carper's games. This was my life he laid in his angry daughter's hands. "Where are you going?"

"Business." He winked at me.

My chest tightened. "I can come with you."

"Like I said, Pero." He narrowed his eyes as if I'd understand a message from one look. "Later."

"You can't leave the girl with me," Cherry called.

"How is Mr. Kilen?" Carper asked pointedly. "Don't tell me you left your husband for Rose."

Cherry folded her arms. "Are you threatening me?"

"Nope. Just reminding you that I know more about your history than you realize. And I can help you escape. You can't possibly prefer Rose's plans for you over Elohim's."

Cherry shook her head. "It's too late to change. What's done is done. Decisions were made."

Carper placed both hands on her arms and smiled.

Cherry leaned back but didn't pull away from his hold.

"New decisions can be made today," he said. "Trust me, *xīn gān bǎo bèi*. I promise this time I won't let you down."

Carper let go and left.

Appearing stunned, Cherry sighed and looked me over again. She walked to the bathroom, started the shower, and threw me a towel. "Get in."

I wasn't going to argue about taking a shower. After Cherry left and closed the bathroom door behind her, I undressed and stepped in, letting the hot water wash away all anxieties.

Cherry called from the room. "I have the perfect dress for you."

Maybe a party would give me and Carper a better chance of leaving without anyone noticing. Kind of like I'd left Moon City. Would I ever see Cathena again? Or Alexis? I never said goodbye. But I hadn't said goodbye to Dad either. I had to see him before finding Mom. Poor Dad. There had to be a hole in the floor where he'd been pacing.

Would Cherry come with us? It seemed like Carper wanted to repair broken relationships between father and daughter and Cherry and her husband who she'd possibly left behind. Perhaps I wasn't the only one to practice forgiveness. I squirted some body wash into my hand and lathered the suds. Wounds from the last month clung to my skin, begging to be scrubbed and washed down the drain.

Not every fall ends with pain.

2

跑步

"Changed my mind." I swiveled on my toes and caught myself before my ankle bent.

Cherry grabbed my arm. "Girl." The word sounded too American for her heavy Mandarin accent. She pulled me to the top of the stairs. "It's only a dress."

I gripped the top of the stair railing, my feet trudging behind me. The sound of mingling and music from a live band made my heart pick up speed. Shimmering chandeliers adorned the foyer, creating a soft and inviting glow. But I hadn't been invited to Rose's party, and I certainly didn't belong.

Cherry looked me in the eye. "I know what it feels like to have Calvin leave you. But if you want to escape, your full cooperation is needed."

Sounded like Jimmy when in the arena, until I didn't cooperate and ran off from Coach Marcus. Would cooperation or defiance keep me alive this time?

"And be confident while you're walking," Cherry said. "You'll bring more attention if you're covering your chest the whole time."

I pulled up the top of my dress to cover the peek of cleavage.

Did it have to be sleeveless? At least the dress came down to my knees. "Why are you helping me get away? Aren't you on Rose's side?"

"At first, when he promised money and a better life in America, but luxury quickly faded. You being here is my chance to leave."

I raised my brow. "You mean you want to go with me and Carper?"

Cherry shrugged.

"Are you sure we shouldn't head back to the room and escape out the window?"

"That is a very bad idea." Cherry shook her head as if she gave a lecture. "You'll fall and break your nose."

I shrugged. "I did it before and lived." I thought back to when I escaped with Henry and Sam from Moon City and we rappelled down the steel wall. "But it made my friend's—I mean, boyfriend's nose bleed."

"See? It's better that you blend in with the crowd. You won't be noticed as much." Cherry held her head high and reached my nose in height. "Now. I want you to repeat after me. I, Pero the chosen."

"Being the chosen isn't that special, you know."

She held a finger out. "Ah. Say it."

I huffed out a breath. "I, Pero the chosen."

"Am sexy."

"I'm not saying that."

"Fine." Cherry sighed. "I'll tone it down for you. Pretty."

"I know that already without needing to wear this stupid piece of cloth."

"That stupid piece of cloth is made of mulberry silk."

I sighed, then scanned the crowd for Rose. If he saw me...

"Have faith, Pero. It's the same thing your mother told me, and I'm saying it to you now."

"But I do have faith."

"You don't show it." Cherry turned. "Now, watch how I walk and copy."

"Are you serious?"

"You're wearing what you Americans would call a knock-out dress. And stop pulling on it. I can't even see anything."

"You can if I do this." I half jumped.

Cherry muttered in Chinese. "Then don't hop, unless you want every guy Rose invited watching you tonight. Which they might still do even though you walk like a penguin."

"That's what I'm afraid of, the guy thing." I straightened my shoulders. "Do I really walk like a penguin?"

It was the heels' fault.

"Whatever you do, stay away from Rose. We need you out of here, whether or not we find Calvin." Cherry grabbed my hand and pulled me from the landing and down the stairs. At the bottom, we weaved through the dancers swaying to the live band playing a bluesy tune. The piano notes escalated my stress of leaving unseen.

Cherry led me through wide open double doors. The music became muffled as we stepped inside a library with walls of books and no one in sight. She shut one door behind her and left the other open a crack. "We'll hide in here for now. I'll keep my eyes open for an escape and see if we find Calvin."

"I only know him as Carper."

Cherry shrugged. "I try to forget my maiden name."

"I don't blame you. Carper's not easy."

"Let's not talk about my father." She peeked through the crack. "Too complicated."

I hid behind the door so if someone walked in, I'd be hidden but hopefully not squished.

Cherry murmured an unfamiliar word.

"By the way you said it, I'm guessing that was a dirty word."

"Shh. I see Rose."

"Thorns and all?"

Cherry glanced at me, her face contorting as if she was annoyed. "Why would you joke at a time like this?"

"Coping mechanism."

"Shoot. He's coming."

No pun came to mind, only the spastic pulse of my heartbeat.

I expected Cherry to call out "See you later," then run, but instead she opened the door wide and marched out. "Rose, there you are. I've been looking everywhere for you. First, I checked the gardens, thinking maybe you had gone for a stroll with Nancy, then into the kitchen where I found the most incredible tiramisu I've ever tasted. You were right to replace..."

"Spit it out, Cherry." The same voice of the man who'd taken Mom, Henry, and Sam graveled. "You're babbling again. I swear, at times you're so much like your father."

Silence followed. I imagined Cherry needed a moment to compose herself after the insult.

"That's the very thing I need to tell you," Cherry said. "Either I'm seeing things, or Calvin Carper was making his way out the door just a moment ago."

This time, the dirty word Rose muttered didn't need a translation. "The front entrance? You're sure?"

"How can I forget my own father's face? Hurry while you have a chance."

Heavy footsteps echoed along to the beat of the music. Another pause, then Cherry closed the door.

"We have one minute, max," she whispered to me. "I'm going to open the door, and we'll escape through the dance floor. Follow me closely, and don't rush. Rose's guards can spot anything off."

I weighed my options: be seen by Rose and in big trouble when he recognized me as the girl who was drugged then hidden in his closet and escaped from him in Moon City, or ignore Cherry's instructions and run. I may have been able to run from Marcus, but there's no way I'd get far wearing heels. My muscles tightened, ready for take off, waddling-penguin style.

"Let's go." Cherry opened the door, grabbed my hand, and strode forward much faster than I anticipated her short legs could take her. "This way."

We bobbed between dancers.

I glanced up to see the entrance ahead and Rose coming through. I gasped at the same time he did a double-take.

"He saw you," Cherry said into my ear.

I could hardly hear with the music blaring and could only nod. *What now?*

Cherry let go of my hand. "Go."

I darted forward, the exit straight ahead. My pulse quickened.

"Excuse me." I weaved around the dancers. My heel caught on the floor, and I fell. There'd be a bruise, but maybe not as lingering as the pounding of my heart.

A guy who looked about the same age as me bolstered my arm.

"You okay?" He lowered his black fedora just above his eyes.

My face warming, I kept my legs together while leaning on his hand to lift me off the floor. Standing tall, the guy's head landed at my chin.

"I'm fine. Thank you." My eyes darted around me. Rose was in view across the dance floor.

"I'm Jace," the guy said. "Want to dance?" His fingers snapped at the end of each sway.

Rose walked in my direction, his eyes drifting between someone else and me. Another man locked eyes with Rose, nodded, and moved in.

Jace bounced on his toes.

"Oh, um, I don't dance."

Cherry pulled on Rose's arm, leaning close to speak into his ear. Rose pushed her away. His face reddened, and his deep voice shook with words I couldn't hear above the trumpet solo. He looked at me.

I had to form a distraction. Be loud. Wasn't that how to scare off a wild animal? I focused on Jace, who twisted and shifted like he'd been born in a jazz club.

"On second thought, I'd love to dance with you."

"Hot socks!" Jace smiled on beat to the snare drum.

Who talked like this? I copied his moves.

"Hey, you're no heeler," he said.

"Whatever that means."

"You're good," Jace said. "What's your name?"

I held back an eye-roll. Sure. Why not allow another guy in line for my number?

Rose pushed dancers out of his way.

"Let's dance over there." I pointed at the front door.

Jace shook his head. "Music's too loud over there. I can barely hear you now."

A guard reached me first.

"Excuse me." Rose's side-kick squeezed my shoulder.

I grimaced.

"She's not available," Jace said.

The man squeezed tighter. Pain shot through my shoulder and my body pulled away.

"You're hurting her." Jace pushed on the man's arm, but the man didn't loosen his hold on me.

"Let her go!" Jace placed his hands on his hips.

The dancers around us paused.

"Is everything okay?" Rose crossed his arms, taking on a wide stance, which for some reason made his hair appear even whiter.

"That man is hurting her," Jace repeated, bringing his hat closer to his eyes as if replicating an intimidating move he'd seen in a movie.

Rose nodded his head. "Let go of her, sir."

The man nodded and let go, a knowing smile on his lips, before leaving the crowd to their dancing. My shaking limbs and twitching cheek didn't tell me whether I'd win or lose this game.

"I'd like to check out your shoulder, Miss," Rose said. "I promise I'll let you dance again in no time."

"I'm fine. No need."

"I insist. You'll be my *chosen* guest." He smiled as he leaned close to my ear. "Pero."

His breath reeked like a strong drink.

I crinkled my nose and pulled away. "I'd rather not."

Rose nodded at Jace. "I'll only be a minute." He hooked his arm through mine and pulled.

I resisted.

"She said no!" Jace shouted and removed his hat, revealing an afro.

The whole room stopped dancing and the trumpet made a sad final note.

All eyes were on Rose who let go of my arm and took a step back. "Everything's okay. Just a little misunderstanding." He circled his arm in the air as if preparing for a grand bow. "Continue."

The piano started with a slower tune. Some dancers left the floor; many more joined.

My date held out his hand, a smile perhaps indicating this was his best opportunity of the evening. Perhaps even the year.

"Can we step outside?" I fanned myself with my hand and hoped the tremble wasn't visible. "I need some air."

"Absolutely."

Had this guy ever dated? Then again, I'd never actually been on a date myself. Kissing Henry in the hallway of a wall didn't count.

Jace placed his hand on my elbow and escorted me through

the double doors and into cool air. I kicked off my shoes, leaned against the balcony, and breathed. I was safe, for approximately two minutes until Rose found another way. More than likely, they were watching my every move. Were there cameras on the roof? Perhaps they zoomed in for a closer look at the sweat marks that trailed down my mulberry silk dress. Maybe they watched me take off my heels, expecting me to run at any minute.

"I'm going to dip the bill," Jace said. "Want one?"

"I don't understand anything you just said."

"A drink." He tipped his cupped hand to his mouth.

"Oh, I'm under age."

He blinked. "It's open bar."

Would I not be carded? "Um, no thank you." I scanned the premise and noticed more guards nearing and watching. "But I'll come with you."

Jace looked down. "Your shoes."

"Right." I slid into them with a grimace. How did Cherry tolerate the equivalent of being stuck in a mouse trap?

"Groovy necklace," Jace said.

The feather had slipped out while I was putting on my shoes. "Thanks." I tucked it back in. Would the necklace work to get me out of here? Where was Carper, anyway?

Inside, mister grip-my-arm-hard watched me as I sat on a bar stool. No, more like growled at me. At least he couldn't touch me yet, but I didn't have much time before he'd find a way.

Jace leaned against the counter and ordered his drink. "You sure you don't want something?"

"Water is fine."

"Absolutely."

The bartender set the water in front of me. When I reached for it, the shaking in my hand was so visible, that I set my hand back on my lap. Panic escalated in my body.

Elohim, what do I do?

I'd won a battle; the wall had fallen, yet I was stuck again with no clear direction out. Carper had all but abandoned me, and knowing him, might forget about coming back.

"This is the wrong drink," Jace said to the bartender. "I asked for a Bee's Knee's. Does no one understand me around here?"

While Jace argued with the bartender, I sensed someone sit at the stool next to me. The spicy-sweet smell of cologne told me it was a man. I kept my head down and occupied my hands by forcing down a sip of water. I didn't want another flirt to run from, nor did I want one of Rose's friends pulling me away.

"A beautiful girl like you can't be too careful." The man's voice was young, maybe twenties, and gentle.

I flushed and couldn't tell if the drops of water on my glass were from condensation or my sweat. Maybe he wasn't talking to me. I turned my head the opposite way, pretending I hadn't heard.

"You know I can see you," he said with a gentleness that reminded me of another guy I knew. "You going to look at me?"

I stole a glance, then my eyes widened, and my breath caught in my throat.

Before I could say a word, the man—whose hair gelled in trendy perfection and who wore dark jeans with a grey tailored jacket that made his eyes a deeper brown—stretched out his hand.

"I'm Sam."

3

隐藏

I tilted my head. Maybe universe jumping altered memories. My hand met his, and as he shook it, a jolt of warm current reminded me of the strong connection between us as two of the chosen. At first, I'd thought it was romantic chemistry, yet the times we'd experienced visions together told me otherwise.

Sam didn't let go of my hand but brought it close to his lips, gave it a quick kiss, and winked. What was that? Either he was more flirtatious than he'd been before, or trying to communicate something.

"Uh, nice to meet you, Sam. I'm—" Should I give him my real name? If this was a game and he was trying to get me out of here, then I needed to act as if we'd never met. Only Rose was aware that Sam and I knew each other. I sensed Rose's sidekick's laser gaze. I swallowed. "My name is Ruth." My middle name.

Sam's posture stiffened, then as if he realized his reaction, he folded into a relaxed, all-American slump. "So, where are you from?" He pursed his lips at the same time I hesitated. If people listened in, TMI could kick me into

Rose's dungeon, or wherever Rose put people he didn't like. Closets, maybe.

"Never mind the small talk," Sam said. "I really want to know if you'd like to dance."

"Hmm. Did that already, and it didn't go so well." How did Sam dance to slow songs? I bet he'd be gentle with his steps and respectful with his hold, unless this flirty Sam was the new thing. Then maybe the new Sam would— *Stop it, Pero!* I belonged to Henry now, and Henry danced better than jazzy Jace any day. So there!

"How about a walk?" Sam asked. "The rose garden in the back is in full bloom."

More than likely planted in Rose's honor, but definitely not for his scent.

I stood and adjusted my dress. "Just what I had in mind."

I hooked my arm through Sam's.

"Hey," Jace called. "Where're you going?"

"It was great to meet you, Jace. Thank you for saving me out there." I pointed to the dance floor.

"You sure you want to go with this guy?" Jace furrowed his brow as if he were preparing to attack Sam with some epic leap. "I'm no dew-dropper."

I nodded as if I understood everything he said. "I'll see you around."

"Absolutely." Jace frowned.

Sam and I walked past the dancers and the library and headed for the kitchen.

"The word *absolutely* has never sounded so sad before," Sam said.

"What are you doing here?" I lowered my voice to a whisper. "Are Henry and Mom here too?"

Rose approached us.

"Uncle Rose," Sam said. "Great party."

That's right. I recalled Sam mentioning something about

Rose being his uncle when we were in the woods at the Lesaries' camp.

"Thank you." Rose tipped his head. "I trust you're aware you're under surveillance."

"Yes, sir," Sam said. "I was about to show her the gardens. Nothing more, sir."

Rose grunted.

Sam placed his hand on the small of my back. "This way."

A chill passed through me. *Just nerves.* Rose would let us go just like that?

Sam pushed me. I tripped, and a maid swerved around me, the tray of food in her hand wobbling back into her palm. As the garden came in full view ahead, Sam opened a door in the hall and shoved me through. I ducked underneath a line of clothes and the hum of two washers and dryers.

My muscles tightened, ready to run.

"Too close, Pero." Sam locked the door and pressed his back against it. "We need to get out of here. Rose knows who you are."

So, Sam did remember who I was, and he'd stop flirting. Then why did I feel disappointed? Duh. Every girl wanted attention. Right?

"Where's Henry and Mom?" I asked.

"Don't know. I came through the closet, but no one else did."

Someone tried to open the door. "Pero?"

"It's Cherry. Carper's daughter."

Sam shook his head. "We can't trust her."

The knocking sounded harder.

"It's okay. She wants to leave with us. She told me this is her opportunity to escape."

Sam grimaced. "I don't know."

"It's clear," Cherry's voice sounded through the door.

I touched Sam's arm. "I don't want to leave her behind."

Sam nodded, then placed a hand on the knob. "Cherry dressed you, didn't she?"

I covered my chest with my hands, wishing the dress had sleeves.

Sam's eyes stayed glued to my face. "I like ordinary Pero better, but you do look exquisite."

Before I could make an awkward reply or interpret the meaning behind the butterflies in my stomach, Sam opened the door, let Cherry in, then closed it again.

"Where were you, Pero?" Cherry glanced at me and Sam, then raised her brows.

My face felt warm.

Sam cleared his throat. "Follow me." He snatched a set of keys from its holder on the wall and opened a door in the back of the laundry room that led outside.

Cherry and I followed.

Sam seemed to know his way around. Without a word, he skirted the perimeters of the house and into a garage. A man in a black overcoat waved.

"Just taking these ladies for a spin," Sam said.

Ladies? Spin? This was not the Sam I knew. Then again, I didn't really know him. Just that he was my first crush and kind of used to be my brother.

"Of course, sir." The man opened the car door.

Sam tossed Cherry the keys. "You're driving." He jumped into the passenger seat. I climbed into the back.

Cherry got into the driver's seat and looked at Sam. "While you're here, I need to teach you how to drive. It doesn't make any sense you never learned while in the U.S."

"Go, Cherry," Sam said. "We don't have time."

She started the engine. "Does she know that you used to live here with your uncle?"

I leaned forward. "Sam mentioned it briefly."

"Go," Sam said.

"Great uncle. Or something like that." Cherry swiveled her head in my direction. "I haven't seen your mom for a long time. Never met her son. And then he just showed up. Yesterday actually."

"Cherry!" Sam shouted.

Cherry pressed on the gas, then slammed on her brakes at the booth in front of the open gate. "Hold on. The guard needs to let us through."

"The gate is open," Sam said. "Just go."

"Better to not make them suspicious." Cherry rolled down her window.

I sank into my seat and dropped my head.

"Hello, Garrett."

"Where are you going?" the guard asked.

The pounding in my heart traveled to my limbs.

"Just taking this young lady back home. She's...not feeling well."

I held back a groan. Maybe I really was sick.

"I'd rather you stay." Rose's voice came from a distance and evoked a chill like an icicle piercing my back. Tucking myself lower, I crouched behind the front seat.

"It won't take us long," Cherry said.

"This isn't a suggestion, Cherry." Rose's voice was closer and lowered an octave. "I need all three of you to stay."

As I remained crouched on the floor, I peeked up to see Rose glaring in my direction. Goosebumps rose on the back of my neck. So much for hiding.

"Uncle. Thank you for welcoming me back home. It's been years since you took care of me after Mom took off and Dad died. You did a pretty good job despite your desire to see me killed. Goodbye."

The car lunged forward. I hit my head on the seat behind me, then noticed Sam had moved his leg to the driver's side. He must've pressed on the gas harder, as we sped over bumps in the driveway. Cherry screamed and turned the wheel when we were inches from a Ferrari.

"Take over, Cherry!" Sam yelled.

Cherry cried. "I can't. Just stop."

"Fine. Stop the car."

Cherry sniffled. The car stopped.

Sam looked back at me. "Pero, you're driving. Hurry."

I ran out of the car and back in.

Sam jumped into the back.

Cherry crawled over to the passenger seat, still sobbing. "I knew this was a bad idea. The whole thing. I can't keep living like this."

"What are you talking about?" I pressed on the gas, out of the long driveway, and onto the highway heading home. My rear-view mirror showed an empty road.

"They won't come." Cherry coughed as more tears fell. "It's all over. And now we can finally forget..."

"Forget what?" Sam rubbed his head.

Cherry scrunched her face. "That Rose paid me to pretend to help her out. Sam taking over wasn't part of the plan." She let out a breath. "There. I said it."

I slammed on the brakes and pulled over. The car screeched, and so did Cherry.

"Pero, keep going." Sam's voice lowered to his usual calm.

"I can't. Not until *that* lady gets out of this car."

Sam turned to look at Cherry. "Why'd you have to open your big mouth right now?"

I looked at Sam. "You knew too?"

"Of course not." Sam grabbed a paper napkin from the glovebox and handed it back to Cherry.

"I really did mean what I said about looking for my escape." Cherry held the napkin against her face and blew her nose. "But Rose keeps dragging me back in with better offers and threats. It's my fault. No, it's my father's fault I'm the way I am."

"You make your own choices." My voice was thick with anger. "Now, are you with me or not?"

Cherry raised her hands in surrender. "I'm in, I'm in. I'll make it up to you. Let me drive, take you home."

I pressed on the gas, and the momentum made Cherry's head hit against the back of my seat. "I drive." My voice roared as loud as the engine from the pressure of my foot on the gas. "From now on."

4

抵达

I pulled into the driveway, parked the car, and stared. This was my house. *My* house.

Sam's hand rested on my shoulder. I thought of nudging his hand away, but instead, I paused. Sam owned land somewhere near here now. Jimmy had given it to him before he died. I could make Green Meadow *our* home. I shook my head to clear the thoughts. I couldn't. I belonged with Henry. I loved Henry.

"As soon as we're in the house," Cherry said, "I'm buying a ticket to China."

"We all are," I said. "And partly because you led Rose right to us."

"Pero," Sam said like a mellow scold and let go of my shoulder.

I ignored Sam's warning, my face heating up as my anger built. "I've spent the last few weeks fighting bad guys, flying on eagles, crumbling walls, falling in—" I cleared my throat. "Now we have to find my mom again, and I don't want anyone in the way with their deception and...and other stupid stuff."

"I told you I'm sorry," Cherry said. "Is that not good enough for you?"

"I've already forgiven your father. I'm not sure how much more hurt I can tolerate." My ears pounded. I stomped out of the car, slammed the door shut, and stuffed the car keys into the front of my dress where Cherry wouldn't find them, just in case she decided to take off to tell Rose our hiding spot.

Sam stepped out.

"Do you think they'll follow us?" I snarled. That's what my anger had to be about. I was scared that I'd be hurt, that I'd experience the same stress on this next trip to rescue Mom.

Sam closed the car door. "Not sure. Cherry thinks Carper paid Rose another large sum to stay put and not follow us."

"Can we really believe that?"

Sam sighed. "I don't know, but we'll figure it out. You should go inside. Focus on finding your dad first."

The blinds from the kitchen inside opened. My breath stalled. Eyes peeked out. The same eyes that didn't notice me sneaking out with Henry and being captured by Jimmy while he paced in front of the same window.

My heart raced as I ran to the front door that opened before I touched the handle. Dad rushed forward and scooped, wrapped, squeezed me, and cried.

"My girl," he said into my ear. "You're here. You're here."

I pulled back and wiped my nose with my bare arm, wishing I still had Dad's sweater. But I had him.

"Pitar." The Old English word for Dad felt the most fitting. It was how I could get closest to him. "I saw Mom, and I know everything about the adoption."

A couple tears dripped down Dad's face.

"It's okay, Dad. She misses you."

Dad clutched my arms. "I loved you from the start. You know that, right? I adopted you because you've always been mine."

I nodded my head. "But there's more."

He wiped a tear from my cheek. "I know that, too, Pero. I just found out that your mom has a son."

I didn't care how he knew. I wasn't Mom and Dad's birth daughter, but at the same time, I always had been. And I was the daughter of Elohim. Cherished and loved.

I looked over to Sam and nudged my head for him to come closer.

He took a couple of purposeful steps forward.

"This is Sam."

I watched Dad's eyes widen in understanding. "You're—? You're Bahar's?"

Sam nodded.

Dad let out a half cry, half laugh. "You must take after your father. You don't look much like her, but I see her eyes."

Sam clapped Dad's back into a hug. "Thank you for being Pero's dad. You mean a lot to her."

Dad's face turned solemn. "You didn't know your mom either, did you?"

Sam closed his eyes for a brief moment. "I have a mom who took care of me. Alexis is her name."

Dad slapped Sam's shoulder. "You have a bigger family now, you hear?"

Sam nodded. "Thank you."

Dad tucked me back into his arm and kissed my head.

So safe. Like being under Elohim's wing. "Dad? I'm never leaving you again. Okay?"

Dad laughed, a pleasant sound that I'd missed. It felt fuller now, like it would've if Mom had never left us. "You *will* leave, but this time, I'm coming with you. And Dr. Carper's coming, too."

I looked up into his face. "How do you...?"

"Hello, Pero."

I faced the doorway. Carper stepped out of the house.

"You devil." I crossed my arms.

"Wouldn't be the first time someone called me that." He crossed his arms too.

"You left without us."

He nodded. "If I stayed, Rose would've found me. Instead, he found money that I left for him and a note saying his work was done."

So, Cherry spoke the truth.

Dad put his arm around my shoulders. "Dr. Carper told me everything."

I cocked my eyebrow. "And you believed him?"

"I wouldn't have if Henry hadn't stopped by to tell me."

I pulled away from his hold. "Is Henry here?"

Dad shook his head. "He left for the airport this morning."

My heart shrunk. I just missed him. "Where to?"

"China," Dad said.

I gulped. "And Mom?"

"Bahar's in China," Carper said. "Right where I put her when she was your age."

Because she'd shown signs of being one of the chosen. That's when Mom's life became meaningful and terrible all at once, when Elohim first called her to be His and Carper tried to steal that calling and make Mom his own.

"Will we be hurt if we go?" Dumb question. Of course, we'd be hurt. But I had to say it out loud to search for some strand of comfort.

Sam stared into my eyes. It didn't feel intimate. It was more that I sensed he cared. "Have you been hurt since you followed Elohim?"

I glanced at Carper.

He turned the other way.

"Yes."

"Have you been betrayed?" Sam asked.

"Yes." Where was Sam going with this?

"Did Elohim hurt you?"

I shook my head. "Never."

"Did He betray you?"

"No, He didn't."

"What did Elohim do for you, Pero?"

"He made a way for the impossible. He kept me safe, under His wings."

Sam smiled. "Don't be afraid or discouraged. Be strong and courageous."

I smiled back. "Shea said that."

This was Sam at the heart. Full of wisdom. Slow to lose sight of faith. I clutched his words, praying for them to remind and direct me. "I'm glad you'll be there."

His smile turned to a frown. "Let's go inside."

He was coming, right? I needed Sam. Or did I? I'd have Henry, if we found him. And Dad. And Mom. And Carper. Not that I cared if he came. And Cherry. *Fine*.

"Uh, where's Cherry?" I scanned the field beyond the house and the driveway that snaked its way to the main road. In the distance, a small figure with shoes in her hand hop-scotched along the driveway. "I'll get her."

Sam stopped me. "No. Your shoes."

Right. A fancy girl's downfall.

Sam caught up with Cherry. She seemed to hesitate, then came back with him.

I would *not* let her come with us. It'd all been a lie. Couldn't we leave her in a closet for someone to find?

As they walked closer, Cherry stopped when she noticed Carper.

"Hi, kid. Missed me?"

I sighed. Of all the things he could've said...

"I'm not ready to talk with you."

Carper crossed his arms. "If we're on the same flight, you may not have a choice."

Cherry grunted.

Sam put a hand on my elbow. "Can I talk with you, Pero?" A shadow fell across his face. "Alone?"

The journey ahead appeared longer than my driveway and further than the ocean we were about to cross.

Carper winked at me.

Yep. Very, very long.

5

去

"I'm not going with you." Sam walked next to me, picking a leaf from a low branch.

I hated goodbyes. I should be used to them by now. But I hadn't said goodbye to Dad when I took off with Carper, nor to Mom the second time she disappeared to Moon City. Both those instances happened quickly. Too much time gave space for one last hug to recognize the parting, like a bandage not ready to be pulled.

"Are you okay?" Sam asked.

"No." Why be dishonest? "I'm tired of people coming and going." Birds flew past and trees swayed from the evening breeze. A time to chill. "But I trust in Elohim."

"Such a change in you, Pero." He stopped walking. "I want to say something that may upset you."

"I'm sure I'll be okay." It couldn't be as bad as finding out I had a brother, then finding out I didn't.

"I think you need to work on forgiving Cherry."

My heart sunk a little. I'd forgiven Carper, maybe too easily and definitely not permanently. "It hurts when someone lets you down. I miss being home with Dad before life got so complicated."

"It's called grief," Sam said. "It's okay to grieve. Part of the way to move forward is to forgive and accept Cherry and Carper for who they are, not who you want them to be."

For some reason, Sam being right didn't irritate me. I couldn't be angry with gentle honesty. "I don't know how."

"It's not immediate. For some it's easy to forgive them and move on. For someone like Carper and Cherry, forgiveness might be a daily choice."

I grinned. "More like hourly at the moment."

"Or hourly. Give it to Elohim. Trust Him in this area like you trust Him to find your mom and Hen—." His words trailed off, but I knew the name he couldn't say.

Henry.

The one I'd chosen to love in a different kind of way. But would we feel the same once reunited? It's not like I'd been in love with Henry for long. Like? Yes. But love was different. A commitment. It felt final. Perhaps I thought I loved Henry when he'd mouthed he loved me from our hiding places behind the trees in Moon City. I regretted I hadn't told him back. But was it real?

Sam stopped walking, and the light reflected in his brown eyes.

"What's wrong?"

He shook his head. "Nothing."

As his hand moved to the back of his neck, my heart flipped before I could remind it that we weren't in gymnastics over this guy anymore.

"It's just..." His hand returned to his side. "We've been through a lot together. I'll miss you."

There it was. The goodbye. I swallowed the lump in my throat. "Come with us, Sam."

He shook his head again with more determination. "There's

land I promised Jimmy I'd take care of. I think that's why Elohim brought me here first, rather than directly to China. Time for me to move on from the past." He paused. "From... from you."

His face turned a lighter pink than the sky. Like he was embarrassed but only a little.

A jolt hit my gut. I needed to move on, too. Not because I was interested in him, but because I couldn't be his friend without him or me wanting more.

Sam glanced my way, then continued walking. "I need to heal. From the grief of my dad, mom, Jimmy."

And me.

"The land will be a good distraction," he said. "Plant something new, you know?"

I blinked back the tears that surfaced. "So, this is goodbye. Like longer than a trip to China kind of goodbye."

His attention lingered on my face as if memorizing every freckle and crease. "Yeah."

"I'll come back. Green Meadow is my home."

But something in his eyes told me the finality of that moment. Even when I did return, it wouldn't be to Sam.

"What about Mom?" I asked. He couldn't go without seeing his own mother once she came back.

"I'm sure I'll see her."

Her. Not me. Maybe he'd see me, but he wouldn't *see* me. Not like he did now.

Somehow, we'd stopped again and the space between us became smaller as his face drew close to mine. I shifted away. Did he expect me to kiss him goodbye? I couldn't.

Sam pulled away. "Let's get back."

He was hurt. And not just from me. I could sense the grief in every step he took. The pain in his face. The squint of his eyes. How had I missed it before? Or was it only when he arrived here, the place Elohim called him next—a place to rest —that he recognized grief?

"Not before I give you a hug." I wrapped my arm around the middle of his back as we walked. Sam's eyes brightened, and he wrapped his arm around me. Our stride was even. The strength from his arm held me up, pushed me on.

The pink sunset changed to yellow. The birds chirped their way past us, flying home.

"I'll miss you too, Sam Nessim."

His strong hand squeezed my arm and released.

6

寻找

The plants had been watered, the floor swept, and Dad sat in the same chair. There was no hole in the path where I'd imagined he'd paced, waiting for me to come home. But more lines creased his face and grey speckled his hair. Or had I not noticed Dad's features as much? Handsome, yes. But older.

"I can't believe you're here." Dad beamed at me. His glider moved in time with the grandfather clock.

I smiled back at Dad from my spot on the couch.

Sam said he'd leave after we were all settled on our next plans. He sprawled out on the floor, right where Henry had. When Henry was here, he'd looked like a surfer with crossed legs, bare feet, and his hair curling near his shoulders. Sam appeared like a lumberjack who didn't belong in the blazer and jeans he'd worn to his grandpa's party. Sam took off his blazer, tossing it next to him. He undid the top button of his dress shirt and loosened his shoulders.

How had I become more relaxed around Sam? As if nothing had happened between us. Sam looked up at me, searching my eyes as if they'd tell him my thoughts. Like he hoped it might tell him something he wanted to hear. That we were...

"Together." I said that out loud. I really said that out loud. Sam's lips curved in a slight smile. I swiveled to Dad, feeling my cheeks warm. "We're all finally together." Awkward.

"A dream come true." Cherry sat on the other side of the couch near me. Her arms crossed, wadded tissue in hand.

"You don't have to join us, you know." I scooted farther from her. "I'm sure Rose would love it if you didn't."

Cherry rubbed her forehead and sighed. "I wasn't expecting my father to be part of my escape."

Dad glanced at Carper who was in the hall, phone in hand with Boon airlines. I eyed the bags lined up in a row near the front door, awaiting our departure: Sam's pack; Dad's grey duffel; Carper's briefcase that he tried to convince us wasn't stolen but borrowed from Mr. Rose's estate; a backpack for Cherry; and my green bag. The same bag that used to be Jimmy's, the one smeared with ancient dirt from another universe and sprinkled with blood. Whose blood? I didn't know. Could have been mine, Jimmy's, Sam's, Carper's. Could've been the remains of the crested blood scattered from those who'd died when the walls crumbled. I shuddered, as if the stain blamed me for Moon City's death and my punishment was to carry it. I should've burned the bag. Started again. But they'd remind me of where I'd been. I wanted to carry that bag with me so that I could remember that if a city's walls could crumble, the beat-up parts of me—the scars from the past I now carried—might one day fade.

"It might not be my place to say this," Dad said, "but it seems to me that if we're going to find Bahar together, then we need to work on being kind."

I looked over at him, expecting his focus to be on Cherry, but instead found it on me.

"Are you talking to me?"

"Yes, but I mean all of us." Dad looked at Carper, then back to me and Cherry. "I know enough about Carper to understand he's hurt us all. Now, I could be bitter about the way he treated my wife and each of you, but that is in the past and it won't help us with our future."

I glanced back at Carper and shook my head. In some strange way, he'd become my friend.

Carper wandered into the living room, his phone held out in front of him. Fuzzy classical music blared on the speaker and a voice said, "Thank you for choosing Boon."

"Finally," Carper said.

"Please continue to hold," the phone said, and distorted music started again.

Carper groaned. "Why is everyone staring at me?"

I shook my head. "Just trying to figure you out."

"But while we're all focused on you," Dad said, "mind telling us what you know about Rose?"

Carper placed the phone on the windowpane leading to the kitchen. "Winter Rose. That's his real name. Don't ask me what his parents were thinking." He looked at Sam. "Well, you're related to him. Do you know what they were thinking?"

Sam raised his brows, then shook his head.

"Rose knows of the prophecy. His father was Bahar's father's cousin. When Bahar first showed signs of being the prophesied chosen, Rose did everything he could to find how he could take her power. So, he did the most reasonable thing possible. Hired me, the world's greatest scientist, the one who'd been experimenting with how to use someone's blood to create undefeatable armies that I called the Warriors."

When I snorted, everyone looked at me. "What? We all know how well that turned out."

"Pero," Dad said. "Be nice, please. I haven't seen this kind of arguing from you since Henry lived here. You two were always bickering."

I glanced at Sam who scratched his chin. I hadn't told Dad about my little fling with Sam, if you could call it that. More like a passing thought. No, it'd been more than that.

"Sorry, Carper. I'm just worked up about finding Mom."

"I understand," Carper said.

Boon Air interrupted with another false-hoped message.

"Rose and I formed a partnership and discovered Bahar's blood was the secret ingredient. We took Bahar from her home, experimented on her. I—." Carper stared at the floor. "Now I'm the one who needs to apologize. I'm sorry, Matthew."

Dad kept his gaze on his thumbs that made circles around each other, hands folded. He couldn't forgive yet. I understood. It took Elohim's act of forgiveness toward me for me to forgive Carper.

Carper sighed. "Pero, I'm sorry for what I did to you and your mom."

"I forgive you." I looked into his eyes so that he could see a heart that was hurt but wanting to move on. Perhaps I could make room to forgive Cherry as well.

"Thank you." Carper bowed his head as if to hide the tears I noticed brimmed his eyes. "Sam, I'm sorry I first took your mom away from you. If it hadn't been for me chasing after her, she might've found you again."

"I forgive you," Sam said, "but don't do it again."

Carper held his hand out. "You have my word."

Sam nodded and shook Carper's hand.

As Carper glanced at Cherry, she turned away.

"Before you continue," Cherry said, "I need to know one thing, and I might as well let everyone hear, to earn their trust and show who they really should be leery of."

Carper scratched his neck, like a nervous twitch.

Cherry's eyes misted. "Did or did not my mother leave me because of you?"

I gasped.

Dad stopped rocking the chair.

Sam stood. "I'll be outside." He headed for the front door.

"Stay." Carper held out his hand to keep Sam nearby.

Sam leaned against the living room wall and folded his arms.

Carper took in a breath and puffed it out. "Cherry, I'm not proud of my past."

Her eyes widened. "How could you? She was the only one who ever loved me."

Carper cleared his throat. "Listen. I hurt you a lot, but I never asked your mom to leave. She did that on her own."

Tears glistened on Cherry's face. "She didn't love me."

I'd told myself the same for fourteen years until I found my own mom. *She didn't love me. If she did love me, she wouldn't have left me.* Then I found her and her love, and I learned it was great enough to love me even though I never was biologically hers. But where was my birth mom? Did *she* love me?

"Maybe she did love you, in her own way." Carper shrugged. "And your husband loved you, at least that's what I remember you saying. Josiah, right? You seemed happy with him."

Dad reached for the tissue box on the end table and handed it to Cherry who took one and wiped her nose and face.

"*Jehoshua* is a good man, but I was scared that it wouldn't last and ran off. Guess I learned the best from my parents."

Carper combed his hair back with his fingers. "I was a jerk. No, I was the son of a word I don't say in front of sixteen-year-olds."

I rolled my eyes. I'd correct my age again, but seventeen-year-olds were more mature than that.

"It will take time to believe me, Cherry, but I am sorry for every stupid thing I did to hurt you. And I'm sorry that your mom took off, more than likely because I didn't love her. I am the one to blame for you not knowing how to receive love."

Cherry stared at the floor as if it could catch on fire and burn away her memories if she looked long enough.

"I won't share any more..." Carper choked on tears, then cleared his throat. "I don't expect any of you to follow me after all I did, but I *am* the only one who knows the whole structure of the Forbidden City."

"Um." Sam rubbed his arm with his hand. "I guess now's a good time to tell you all that I'm not going."

A thump beat in my chest, and my hand flew there. Why couldn't I let Sam go?

"I'm not going because I need—"

"Thank you for calling Boon Air. This is Bonny. How can I help you?"

Carper grabbed his cell and turned off the speakerphone. "Yes, Bonny of Boon. My name is Calvin Carper and I need five —no four—tickets to Beijing immediately."

Pause.

"...First class... Yes, tomorrow morning works... Yes, Calvin Carper is spelled just like the famous scientist." Carper winked at me. "You know, not a lot of people have asked, but I also haven't traveled the world in a while."

Ten minutes later, Carper hung up. "It's done. I've got fake passports for all of us." Carper tossed each of us a little blue book. "One of Rose's shady businesses came in handy this time."

"When did you have time for this?" I asked.

"I may have snuck into his counterfeit room," Carper said.

"You never had one of those in your mansion."

"How do you know?" Carper lifted his brows.

I opened the book, and a picture of me smiling—my brown hair hanging at my shoulders—looked back. "Where'd you get my school picture?"

"Come on, Pero. You can find anything on the internet."

"That's creepy."

"Why don't you all take one of Carper's pills?" Sam asked. "The ones with the *li* plant that makes you fly."

"Better than taking a slow boat to China," Dad said.

I smiled.

"Can't," Carper said. "I need Abram blood, and since Pero's not related to Bahar..." Carper looked at Sam. "Wait a second."

Sam shook his head. "No, no, no. You're not taking my blood for your experiment."

Carper pulled out a needle and a vial from his pocket. "Please? It's only an experiment."

"You seriously were going to take those on an airplane?" I asked. "And who carries vials in their pockets?"

"I stuffed them in my pocket when I found them among the rubble in Moon City." Carper held the needle out and raised his brows at Sam.

"Fine, but at least wash your hands first."

Carper smiled. "Smart man." Putting away the tools, Carper disappeared into the kitchen, then returned a couple minutes later with hands lifted. "Washed, twice."

Sam offered his finger. "Just one small...ouch."

Carper squeezed Sam's finger till his blood dropped into the vial that already held a green liquid. "Pero, you drink it."

I stepped back. "Who do you think I am? A vampire?"

"You try it first," Dad said to Carper.

"Okay." Carper didn't hesitate to take a sip of the liquid. His face distorted. "Nasty."

We waited. Nothing happened.

"Maybe I should take another sip." Carper held the vial to his lips.

Cherry screamed.

Carper jumped. "What was that about?"

I pointed at Carper. "You're...you've—"

"You grew." Sam's lip quivered as if he were trying to hold

back a laugh. "I may be an Abram, but my blood must not be the same as Bahar's. Neither is my gift the same."

Carper patted his stomach which had been as flat as Stanley before but was now round. His cheeks swelled. "Explain?"

"I make things grow," Sam said.

I laughed until my body bent over. Dad laughed more at me than the situation. Sam grinned, and Cherry blasted Chinese at Carper.

"Laugh all you want." Carper shrugged. "It'll wear off by tomorrow."

7

选

Cherry snored while sleeping on the floor, despite the guitar strings vibrating under my fingers, tinging at every pluck. I laid my head back against the closet wall. When I squinted, the twinkle lights glimmered like stars.

As Elohim's children, we are like stars, Sam once said. *So many, yet each just as spectacular in its brightness.*

But one star couldn't light up the sky without the others. Kind of like I couldn't shout down a wall without many voices and I couldn't find Mom without Carper.

There was a tap, and the door opened.

"It's me," Dad whispered. "Why are you still awake?"

The strings hummed as I placed my guitar on the floor. Dad plopped next to me on the purple cushion. His shoulder was a perfect height for me to lay my head on. What would happen when Dad left too? Maybe not then, but someday. Familiarity couldn't be my security.

"I don't know where I belong, Dad."

"What do you mean, hon?"

"I love being home, even for one night, but my life is different now. All these years, I've waited for Mom to return so

I'd be happy. But now that I've met Elohim, I don't think satisfaction comes from having our family together. Sam's planting his garden, Carper's out to save the world, you're getting out of the house for the first time in a century, and Cherry...not sure about her." Dad rubbed my neck as I strung my words together. "I want to be where I'm needed. When we come back home, I don't want to stay in a small closet playing my guitar. I want to do something important."

"Is that what Elohim's asked you to do?"

"I don't know what He wants. He hasn't talked to me lately."

"Why do you think that is?"

Cherry shifted in her sleep and muttered, "They don't have that."

I chuckled and spittle flew out.

"Sorry, Pero," Cherry muttered, then snored again.

I wiped my mouth, the smile fading from my lips. I hadn't heard Elohim's voice because I wasn't listening. Because I was too focused on Cherry hurting me. I didn't like it when people I trusted let me down, which was why I'd shut people out before. But that wasn't me now. Sam was right. I needed to forgive. "I'll talk with Cherry tomorrow."

Dad kissed my head, then stood. "Get some sleep."

"Pitar?"

Dad smiled.

"I thought your professor mind was too smart to believe in God."

"That was before He brought you back to me. Don't lose your faith, Pero. Doesn't take much to see you've changed in a good way. I need your gift of faith. I think wherever you bring it is where you belong."

"Goodnight." I crawled into bed, leaving the twinkle lights on. *Be the brightest, Elohim. Lead the way.*

One light blinked as if Elohim was a wishing star melding into my heart, warming, settling, making me its home.

8

跟随

Explosions filled the screen.

"Yes!" I lifted my hands in celebration.

We all sat in a row in the middle aisle: Carper, Dad, me, Cherry.

Dad leaned over to look at the screen in front of me. "Won again?"

"Fourteen hours of flying." I stretched. "That's lots of time to practice my Goober Smash skills."

Carper sat up and leaned past Dad. "Fourteen hours and fifty-six minutes." He rubbed his head. "And there's no such thing as a Goober Smash skill. I really wish you'd take a break from that dumb game, Pero. I'm trying to sleep."

"Maybe the problem is you're sitting upright."

"That's the only option in economy." Carper shifted. "If Boon Air knew who they were talking to, they'd have given me first class and stuffed some industry fancy-pants or high-end fashion model into this so-called seat. Must be as hard as the Chinese emperor's throne."

"Are we going to meet the Chinese emperor?" I asked.

Carper gave one hardy laugh. "There hasn't been an emperor in over a hundred years."

Seated between us, Dad closed his eyes, a sign that he wanted nothing to do with the discussion.

"Oh." I sat back. "Well, *I'm* having fun."

"You call this fun?" Carper asked.

"It's my first time on a plane."

Carper shook his head. "I still can't believe that."

Jitters exploded in my belly like candies in the game. "What will it be like when we get there?"

"Stop worrying," Carper said. "Like I said, I have the Forbidden City memorized."

"Is the Forbidden City similar to Moon City?"

Dad's head drooped as if he was really sleeping instead of faking.

"What makes you think that?" Carper asked.

"I don't know. Maybe because they both have the word *city* in them and because you came from both."

Cherry touched the screen and unplugged her earbud. "Pero, didn't you ever watch the documentary, *Dr. Carper's Forbidden Lab*?"

"Are you serious?" I leaned past Dad. "You really are a big deal, Calvin."

"You're mocking me."

I laughed.

Dad jolted. "You want me to trade places so you two can talk?"

"No!" Carper and I said at the same time.

Carper folded his arms and muttered.

"I can't hear you."

He leaned over Dad. "I said I'll give you a tour. Underground style. We'll sneak into an off-limits hidden entrance and find a way to get Bahar and Henry."

"Won't someone recognize you?"

Carper pointed to the white-bleached wig he put on that morning.

I rolled my eyes. "Oh, you're *so* disguised."

"Worked in Moon City," he said.

"That's because they were distracted by my bright yellow hat."

"I have the hat still, too. Let me know when you need it."

I crossed my arms and leaned back into my chair. "Never again."

Dad squeezed my knee.

"Sorry," I relaxed my shoulders.

Cherry laughed from the seat next to me.

I opened one eye to see her watching the screen in front of her, then closed it again. I still hadn't talked with her. Maybe she'd stay on our side if I were nicer. I could write a note. Reaching into my bag, I found a crumpled napkin wadded up with gum. No pen. I breathed out a sigh. I'd have to tell her.

"Whattcha watchin?" I asked. On her screen, Indie talked with his ex-lady in the latest *Indiana Jones*.

Cherry paused the show. "Oh, now you're talking to me?"

"I was before." My face heated up. "Cherry, I'm sorry for everything. I've been a pain in the you-know-what."

Cherry's lips curled into a tight smile. "I kind of like you, Pero, and I need to work on liking people again."

She seemed kind and considerate when not clouded with fear. I understood that. Had I judged her too quickly without knowing who she was behind the scars?

The flight attendant strolled by with a trash bag. I handed him the napkin. As he took it from me, he held on and tightened his grip for a second before putting the trash away. I shivered as I looked into his eyes. Tilting my head, I tried to figure out if I knew him, but my recollection didn't bring anyone to mind. His eyes stayed on mine, a vacant stare, until he left our aisle.

Shivering, I turned to Cherry who hadn't noticed the exchange. Who was that? And why had he looked at me as if he had something to say?

I stretched, then unbuckled my seatbelt. "I'm getting in line for the restroom."

"Best of luck. Last time, I stood there for ten minutes."

It'd be good for me to move. I got up, careful to not hit my head on the luggage compartment above me, and shuffled past Dad and Carper.

At the same time, Carper and I held out a peace sign with two fingers, then glared while pointing them to our own eyes and then the other's.

"I've got my eyes on you, kid."

I stuck out my tongue, then stepped forward and nearly bumped into the person in front of me. Crossing my arms, I raised my brows at Carper. "Looks like the end of the line is right next to you."

"Just when I was finally going to take a nap."

"No one's stopping you, man."

He crossed his arms, closed his eyes, and settled back. "Sure."

I shook my head, failing every attempt to hide a smile. Carper might be a bajillion years older than me, but at least he appreciated my kind of humor.

Five minutes later and half-way through the line, singing filled the plane. I looked to the ceiling and at every speaker around me. Was the pilot singing? That would be very strange. No one else seemed to notice. They all kept their gazes focused on their screens or books or drooled on their neighbor's shoulders.

The singing continued. A woman's voice. Delicate and beautiful.

"Do you hear that?" I asked the tall man in the business suit who stood in front of me.

He looked over his shoulder. "It's the hum of the engine, miss." He turned back to the line that moved forward three steps.

It wasn't a hum. I strained an ear to hear the words, but it was too distant to understand. Maybe a passenger decided to sing to pass the time, or cloud sirens existed and flew through the sky, enticing pilots and their crew to join them. Didn't sailors drown from following mermaids? I blinked. I'd been on this plane too long. Flying mermaids? So not valid.

Minutes later, a breathtaking melody still filling the air, I arrived to the front of the line.

"Psst."

I glanced around, nothing appearing out of the ordinary. Sheesh, I was hearing voices again.

The flight attendant who'd given me the creepy stare stepped from behind the curtain where staff loaded cookies and carbonated beverages.

I jumped and stepped on the toe of the person behind me. "Ouch."

I turned to the woman. "I'm so sorry. Are you okay?"

"I'm nearly eighty years old. Of course I'm not okay. Teens have no respect for the elderly these days."

"It was an accident. It's my first time on a plane. I'll tell you what, I'll give you my next snack."

She rolled her eyes. "Forget it."

The tall man who'd waited in line in front of me stepped out of one of the restrooms.

"I'll let you go next," I said to the woman.

She rushed forward. "I'll agree to that. Just wait, girly. One day your bladder will be weak like mine."

I did not need to hear that.

The creepy flight attendant stepped near me as if to pass by, then paused when we were side by side. "Elohim wants you to follow the voice."

I yanked back, eyes wide, heart beating overtime. "Where?"

He shook his head. "That's all I heard. Follow the voice."

He walked briskly down the aisle. I kept my gaze forward long after he'd disappeared, noticing the engine's hum when the singing had silenced. *Follow the voice.* What did it mean?

A tap on my shoulder woke me from my stupor.

"It's your turn, miss." It was the woman whose toe I'd stepped on.

I cleared my throat, and after sliding the door to the laboratory behind me, imagined being sucked down the toilet and to the chilling arms of the sirens who lived in the clouds or ocean. Didn't matter which, as long as Elohim was the one who'd put me there. If the voice did lead me to captivity, I'd rather not be alone.

9

进入

On sidewalks, shoppers huddled around cloth strung along poles and tables of slippers. Hello Kitty winked at me from a pink shirt. Louis Vuitton bags hung by the hundreds.

"Those bags are fake," Cherry said from the taxi's seat next to me. "So are the name-brand clothes. They call it black market shopping. I call it jackpot shopping."

The car moved forward, then stopped, jerking my head.

Carper asked from the front seat. "Why buy fake Puma when you're wearing a real one?"

Cherry looked at her jacket, then back at Carper. "Fake."

Carper smiled. "You fooled me."

"What's that?" Dad craned his neck to look out the window.

I followed Dad's gaze and where a burnt-red wall rose so high I strained to see the top. "Is that the Great Wall?"

"Ha!" Carper said something to the driver in Chinese, then glanced in our direction. "The only thing that makes it great is it's where we're headed."

"The Forbidden City," Dad said.

Crowds lined the sidewalks, waiting to cram into what must've been the entrance.

We drove past.

"Aren't we stopping?" I asked.

"You expect us to march in there without anyone noticing?" Carper asked. "Armed guards surround this place, and they'll recognize me."

"Maybe your bleached hair will fool them."

Carper patted the tips of his hair. "They'll know."

I snorted. "You should've borrowed my yellow hat."

Dad scowled at me, and I answered with a shrug. He'd be surprised how much I'd teased Carper the last couple of weeks. Then again, if he knew how much Carper sassed me, he'd relax a little more. "Where *are* we going?"

"Tiananmen Tower," Carper said, "where we can see the entire palace."

"The gate of heavenly peace," Dad said. "It's 66 meters long, 32 meters high."

Carper raised an eyebrow at Dad.

"He's a history professor," I said. "More facts to come. Believe me."

"I bet your history books never mentioned the hideouts," Carper said to Dad. "The part of the Tiananmen Tower we're going to is tucked away from the crowds."

"You're sure the guards don't know about it?" I asked.

"They don't know I've got your necklace. That's all I need."

I rolled my eyes. "The necklaces don't work, remember? And I'm not really Abram blood."

Carper raised a finger to his lips and glanced at the driver who was busy honking at a swarm of pedestrians passing by.

"Don't say the 'A' word," Carper said. "He doesn't speak English, but that word. It's code."

Right. Because the Abram family was chosen. Because their blood was special. My stomach fluttered. Maybe it was good Sam wasn't here. One less person to worry about being caught.

"My plan will work." Carper rolled back his shoulders. "Trust me."

Somehow, I did.

The driver pulled onto a sidewalk in front of a tower blocked by an iron gate. Carper handed the driver a bill with a portrait of a person's face. It was the same face I noticed hanging on the red wall inside Tiananmen Square. Dad had mentioned who he was. Mao-something. And what had he called the money? *Yuin? Yuán?* Maybe I'd know more if I paid attention to Dad's history fetish. The only historical fact I could remember was about a cat who'd survived three sinking ships during his naval service in World War II. How's that for important?

We got out of the taxi, and Carper led us to the red wall. He studied it from different angles and scanned the premises as if unsure he'd be caught. "This isn't it."

"What isn't it?" I asked.

We followed him a few more paces.

Dad stopped to look up at the tower, probably wondering how he could apply the sights to next term's class.

The tower resembled pictures I'd seen of pagodas, a structure made of what looked like stacks of pyramids on top of each other.

Cherry grabbed a pack of gum from her purse and shoved a piece into her mouth. "Want some?"

"What flavor?" I asked.

Carper scanned the wall and crowds. Was he sniffing?

"Giraffe Speckle."

Carper pounded his fist around the brick wall. He was losing it.

"What the heck is Giraffe Speckle?" My eyes still fixed on Carper.

Cherry pressed something in my hand. "It's coffee flavored with spots of chocolate."

I grimaced. "Sounds disgusting and good at the same time." I unwrapped the gum and put it in my mouth. "It's...very—"

"Aha!" Carper scurried over. "Pero, I need your necklace, and you three were supposed to be watching out for me."

I shrugged. "Looked like you were doing that already."

"Sorry," Dad said. "This architecture is so intricate."

I narrowed my eyes at Carper as I gnawed on the gum.

Carper held out his hand. "The necklace, please."

I shoved my hand to the bottom of the bag where I'd hid it underneath rolled-up clothes and handed the broken necklace to Carper.

"Oh, yeah." Carper's lips pouted. "Forgot you broke it. Hope it still works."

He pushed the pieces of the feather pendant together, and they stuck. The necklace was now whole again. Why hadn't I tried that? He inserted the feather into a crack of the wall.

We waited, my heart beginning to pound. I looked at Cherry who shrugged at me. After several silent moments, Carper reached for the wall just as it made a *click* sound.

"When you have a key," Carper said, "a door waits."

"Sounds like a fortune cookie."

"The entrance is around the corner." Carper led us to a nook in the wall. No door in sight. Carper pushed on the brick wall, and it swallowed him whole.

"What the..."

"Where did he go?" Dad looked at Cherry.

Cherry shook her head. "I know very little about my father and his secrets."

"Must be Hogwarts style." I stepped forward. "I'll go next."

Dad shook his head. "Impossible."

"Just you wait, Dad. With the feather, Elohim, and faith, things might get weird."

As I stepped through the wall, it warped around me painlessly. I ended up on the other side, my eyes fluttering in the dimness.

"That was sick!"

My eyes adjusted to the low light. Wooden steps spiraled up. Centered above me and from the top of a circular structure, a large bell hung. Light poured in from windows at the top. Behind me, Cherry and Dad appeared through the wall, which closed right behind them.

"Incredible." Dad examined the wall as if a posted sign would explain the history of wall traveling.

We followed Carper up a spiraling and crumbling stair case. The steps that remained creaked under our weight. Wooden columns supported each level, and beams and brackets joined the columns. A sign near the stair case in Chinese characters and in English read, "Take care of your head." Each storey held verandas with banisters, but we didn't rest at any until we reached the steeple at the top. We all doubled over, panting.

Dad approached a sign near the railing facing the open center where the bell hung from the ceiling. He leaned closer to the Chinese characters as if that would help him understand how to read Mandarin. "What does it say?"

Carper approached the sign. A small window's light illuminated the words: *Ring the bell*.

"Ooh." I put a hand on the suspended wooden beam that aimed toward the bell.

"Don't do it. Legend says whoever hears this bell ring has found the chosen. They'll chase you."

Dad tilted his head. "I thought Buddhists ring bells for the sound to reach heaven and to remind listeners to pray for peace."

"We're in a hidden pagoda in the Tiananmen Tower," Carper said. "It may have been designed for Buddhists originally, but Elohim has hidden this specific pagoda from those after the three chosen." Carper nudged with his head. "Come take a look."

The balcony narrowed so we each had to squeeze our way to the opening and cram to see. Around the perimeter of the Forbidden City lay forested land. Beyond the hedge, thousands of buildings and skyscrapers appeared grey against the palace's yellow-tinted roofs.

"It's bigger than Moon City," I said.

Carper frowned. "Bigger and just as terrible. I'm not proud of what I made in the labs of this city."

Dad pointed. "The roofs are interlocked, which is how they've survived about 2,500 years. Yellow is said to be imperial, which is why they used yellow for most of the roofs during the Ming and Qing dynasties. See the green on some of the roof tiles?" Dad pointed. "Green signifies growth and was used on the prince's quarters."

"Everything is symmetrical in China," Cherry said.

"A perfect puzzle." Carper took in a breath, then paused. "In Shanghai, a garden has a pagoda similar to this one." Was that a tremor in his voice? "My mother and I used to climb it when we visited...my father."

I could only guess what Carper's mother was like. Did she raise him to be kind? All I remembered hearing about his childhood was that he was raised a Lesarie and didn't like the rules.

"At the top of that pagoda in Shanghai is a bell," Carper said. "My mother and I used to take turns ringing it. But one year when I rang it, the legend came true. The soldiers waited for us at the bottom of the pagoda. I'm not one of the chosen three, but I could see visions. They took me, wanted to make money off of me from my science experiments." Carper cleared his throat.

"I didn't know that," Cherry whispered.

Carper's expressionless face gazed forward. "There's a lot about me you don't know."

We stayed quiet for a moment. Did *anyone* have a happy beginning before being caught by heartache? Or did Elohim allow the difficult to make us stronger? Pain seemed unavoidable, like a virus waiting to attack. Yet we survived.

"I have a point to this story," Carper said. "From the top of the pagoda in Shanghai was a view of the garden. On the four corners adjacent to the pagoda were four perfectly-manicured bushes in green and maroon, shaped like dragons. They told a tale. They solved a puzzle."

He studied each of our faces, as if we would understand what this story had to do with the pagoda we now stood in.

"Are you saying the Forbidden City's layout is a puzzle?" Dad asked.

Carper smiled and nodded.

I scanned the landscape below me. No dragons. No hidden message like there'd be in an escape room. Just rows of symmetrical paths.

"I see it." Dad pointed his finger. "Lines point horizontally and vertically to make a pattern."

"Sometimes we focus so much on the objects around us," Carper said, "that we forget to look at the space between. The white spaces will tell you where you really are."

Another fortune cookie. I squinted, as if before me was one of those three-dimensional pictures with a hidden image.

"Oh!" Cherry moved in closer. "It's a Chinese character."

"All I see is cement." I moved to where Cherry stood and tried to see from her angle, not that I could understand it if I had seen.

"Pero knows what it means," Carper said.

Everyone looked at me. I blinked. "I can't even see the dang thing."

"You wear it every day."

I gasped. The Lesarie word for *strength*. "Koach?"

Carper nodded. "In Chinese, we say, *liliàng*. It means power."

Dad scratched his chin. "The Forbidden City represents power, a gift from Heaven, and the center of the world."

"It does on the outside," Carper said, "but the buildings are constructed so that those who see from this pagoda, at this specific angle, remember *Who* everything is built on. And if you look on the other side of the bell, you'll see the same word." Carper pointed to another character on the bell. "*Lìliàng*. Strength."

"Elohim's power," I said. "How do you know all this?"

"From me." A figure emerged from the shadows and into the light.

10

唱

The man's black robe landed mid-calf, and a round hat sat a top his curly hair. A Lesarie priest. He stroked his bushy beard, then bowed his head at Carper. "*Nǐ hǎo*, Calvin."

Carper bowed his head in return. "Josiah."

"It's Jehoshua."

"You aren't killing me," Carper said, "so we must be on good terms."

"I'd never kill you, Calvin." Jehoshua smiled, revealing straight, white teeth. He spoke something in Mandarin, then his laughter roared, a sound I'd never heard from a priest when I attended sanctuary in Green Meadow.

Carper's cheek twitched.

"What did he say?" I asked Carper.

"He said he'd hit me as soon as the opportunity comes."

I'd wanted to hit Carper many times, so I couldn't blame him.

The priest looked me in the eye, then bowed his head. "I am Jehoshua Kilen, priest of the Lesaries in a Chinese sanctuary."

I returned his bow. "Pero Moshe. This is my dad, Matthew. And

Cherry..." I stopped introducing when her face turned two shades of red. Cherry had mentioned this man's name earlier. If I remembered correctly, Jehoshua was the husband Cherry left behind.

Cherry cast her eyes to the floor, then took a quick glance. "How are you, Jehoshua?"

The priest's face hardened but still appeared open, as if he couldn't decide if he should walk away or embrace her. "Fine. Just fine."

"We need to talk." Cherry lifted her gaze. "Later."

The tension between them was thick.

"If that's what you want."

Carper cleared his throat. "Random fact that Jehoshua will appreciate. Pero is an Abram."

"Actually, my mom is an Abram."

Jehoshua raised his brows, which made them look bushier. "Bahar."

Dad stepped forward. "Where is she?"

Jehoshua shook his head. "I'm sorry. I don't know where she is."

I wanted to ask if he knew someone named Henry, but the question wasn't worth the embarrassment.

"You may all follow me," Jehoshua said. "This is an underground sanctuary, which means our spot must stay a secret. If the government finds us in here, we will be persecuted."

Inside what? The Emperor's Palace? We were at a dead end, unless another door hid somewhere in the wall.

"Carper," Jehoshua said. "The Lesaries won't be happy to see you."

Carper nodded.

Jehoshua hesitated as if weighing his words. "You look different. Bruised face, no gold earring, white hair. What happened?"

Carper rubbed the bandage on his head that no longer

needed to be there. The blood from his fight against Moon City's guards had long dried. How would he explain? Overnight, he'd become an Elohim-following, babbling, annoying man. Well, the likable kind of annoying.

"I believe in Elohim." Carper didn't choke on his words. No shame. "And I owe you an apology."

I swiveled to Jehoshua to gauge his response.

"I had to hear it to believe what I sensed." Jehoshua dipped his head toward the shadows where he'd stepped from. "There's a young man this way who you all know."

I gasped. Henry?

Jehoshua cocked an eyebrow, and my cheeks blazed. Why was everyone staring at me?

"He hasn't stopped talking about this Pero girl." Jehoshua winked, then reached the pagoda's nook in the shadows.

Henry was here! I grabbed Dad's hand.

Jehoshua pushed on a brick that moved, revealing a dark stairway dimly lit from below. Yep, another secret door. He stopped and turned. "Remember to keep silent about our hiding place."

Dad squeezed my hand back. I didn't know if we were closer to finding Mom, but I sensed we were about to find another world. Maybe not a different physical planet, but a safe place, behind another wall.

WHEN JEHOSHUA TOLD us that behind the secret door was a hidden sanctuary, I'd pictured people huddled together in fear and whispering prayers. A party was far from my mind. People laughed and chatted. Others watched someone singing karaoke on a stage and cheered when the voice sang out about heartache.

Carper nudged me with his elbow. "Isn't that your boyfriend on stage?"

I looked for a blonde head in a sea of black hair, then noticed him in the center of the stage, a mic in hand. I took in his shoulder-length sandy locks. His head drew back as he bellowed in laughter. That smile. Those blue eyes that met mine, brightening in the stage light.

"Pero." My name blared from the speaker pulled me forward. Henry set the mic down and jumped off the stage. Ignoring the crowd's stare, I rushed into his open arms. I breathed deeply the familiar scent of citrus and a foreign spice, perhaps fennel.

"Join me in karaoke?" he asked in my ear. "I kind of left the crowd hanging on a 90's pop song."

I settled from the comfort of his voice and nodded hesitantly as if I agreed with such craziness. Join him in karaoke? When I sat next to him in the car the last day of school, I never imagined I'd be singing with him on stage on the other side of the world. That day, as he'd danced in the car and asked me to sing along, I shrank back. He'd said I was hard to reach. Yet here—and now—my heart was open.

"*The Backstreet Boys* are old," I said.

"They're as charming as me." He winked.

I laughed, grabbed his hand, and marched to the stage. The crowd hollered. What had I gotten myself into?

The music faded.

"I guess the song is over," I said to Henry.

"Sing! Sing!" The crowd chanted. "Sing, sing, sing!"

"I choose a song for you," said a man near the karaoke machine with a grin stretching between his full and round cheeks. "You like this song."

Henry shrugged. "This is China, baby."

Right. Go with the flow.

A soft flute began, and I groaned as the crowd hollered even louder.

"I don't know this song," Henry said.

"It's also old." I smiled.

"Very long intro," he said.

"Just follow along." I sang into the mic.

Henry watched me, his blue eyes sparkling in wonder. I turned and let my gaze stay on the screen that guided me to each word of the song. I couldn't look at him. It was too close. How could I publicly show my emotions when I didn't even know what to do with them? A hug felt more comfortable than a kiss, but did I really want to kiss him again? Isn't that what couples were supposed to do? Then why did it feel like pesky flies buzzing in my stomach rather than dreamy butterflies? As if a few days' distance had made him like a brother to me again. I liked him. Maybe even loved him. Yet, something wasn't in sync. Without a kiss, without a "dating" label, without a commitment to anything serious, he was just my funny friend, Henry. What did that mean for us?

"*Near,*" I sang.

"*Near,*" Henry echoed.

I half-laughed, half-sang, "*Far,*" and Henry repeated. He tried to echo the next line, but I interrupted him as I kept singing.

I heard Dad's roar of laughter from the crowd. Dad was excited when I told him about me and Henry, but he wasn't surprised. Said that as much as we argued, he always thought we'd be a good fit. Dad liked to laugh, but the years without Mom had choked his humor. If Henry brought Dad's laugh back, maybe he was the best thing for me. When Mom came back, we could be a normal family. A happy family.

When the music died, a chant echoed across the room: "Kees, kees, kees."

"What does 'kees' mean?" I looked quizzically at Henry.

Henry grinned at me. "They're saying 'kiss.'"

My face flushed. "No, no, no." I buried my face in my hands.

He laughed. Of course, he wasn't embarrassed. Henry was right at home as the center of attention.

A woman sang in the background loud enough to be noticed.

"Who's singing?" I asked.

I remembered the flight attendant's words. *Follow the light.* My skin felt clammy.

Henry whispered near my ear. "Should we make the crowd happy, Pero?"

The voice grew louder, as if she was singing into my other ear.

I put a hand to his shoulder and gently pushed him away. "I'm not joking, Henry. Who is that?"

I looked around for the source. The melody, so familiar. I knew this song.

"There are voices everywhere," Henry said, his arm gesturing to the packed room.

But this was different. And as more notes flowed, I remembered where I'd heard it.

Mom.

Sing her song. Sam's voice spoke in my thoughts, at least it seemed to be Sam. Elohim's voice was much deeper—clearer. But Sam's was calm, alluring, and very...human. Why and how was Sam talking to me?

A vision.

I looked around and noticed that everyone had stopped chanting, gazing at me with blank stares. They waited for something, and it wasn't a kiss. Henry slowly stepped back. My eyes met Carper's. He nodded, like he knew what I heard. So, he still had the gift of hearing the visions. And for some reason, Elohim still chose me to carry a gift of song even though I was not the two of three chosen.

Next to Carper, Jehoshua shifted slightly, tears trailing down his cheeks and a bright smile directed at me. What did he know?

All *I* knew was to sing. With Mom's lullaby in mind, I let a breath in, then out, and brought the mic to my lips. Mom had sung it to me when I was a baby and again when we were with the Lesaries in the camp. I'd laid my head on her lap, and she shared this song, the same one Elohim—for some unknown reason—wanted me to sing to the sanctuary.

The words gradually began to come back. "Do not worry about tomorrow. Don't you worry about today."

A picture flashed before my eyes. A baby tucked in a blanket underneath a tree. She didn't cry. A woman reached for her but didn't lift her.

I sang, my voice growing stronger with each word.

"My child, I love you, and I am your King."

When a comforting presence hovered over the baby, I felt it settle. The woman reached again for the baby—for me.

I sang the last line.

"Even in your suffering, even in your pain, even in your discomfort,
I am who I am."

Faces flashed before me: Mom, the baby, and another woman, but it was so quick I couldn't catch who.

The vision ended. I blinked before the crowd who watched me. Hushed murmurs waved across the people.

"The chosen," I heard from the crowd. "The one."

Henry grabbed my hand and held on. I lifted the mic to my lips once again, swallowing my fears.

"I'm Pero." I took a deep breath. "The chosen."

I don't know what lead me to tell them. I wasn't sure of it

myself. But it seemed that Elohim had something in mind for me and these people. Excited voices grew.

"To King Elohim!" Jehoshua shouted.

"To King Elohim!" the people echoed. Lifting their hands, they wept.

11

计划

The sound of shuffling feet and muted voices outside my room woke me. Rubbing my eyes, I sat up to look at the clock on the wall. Ten minutes till eight. Breakfast. I jumped out of bed, brushed my teeth at the small sink, and pulled on the khaki shorts and white t-shirt a woman laid out for me the night before. One look in the hand-held mirror made me grimace. A toothbrush and toothpaste had been packed, but not a brush. Figured. I'd survived Moon City without one, so I could make it work again. Combing my fingers through my hair, I dug for a hair tie in my bag. At least it wouldn't be a complete disaster.

The single room they gave me last night wasn't bad. Not as nice as the Moon City rooms Carper had kept slaves in, but it included the basics: sink, toilet, a bamboo mat on a low bed frame. Darkness shrouded the small space. The wooden walls appeared ancient from the glow of a single lightbulb hanging from the ceiling.

Okay, so it wasn't much to look at, but the people made it feel like home. The Lesaries invited me as family, both Shea and his clan in the other universe, Origo, and here in China, hidden under a famous landmark. Elohim made us family, like He was our Father and we His children, united as brothers and sisters.

The previous evening had been strange, in a good way. The Lesaries wept from the lullaby I sang, but also because their prayers had been answered. It seemed I was the fulfillment to their prophecy, and even though I had said the words out loud, I didn't understand why. Was it Elohim's plan all along to include me as one of the three chosen? The Lesaries said I'd rescue them from the sanctuary underground. But how?

In the vision, Sam talked to me, which had never happened before, and a voice sang. Unknown, yet important. I could sense it.

I glanced at the clock. Two minutes till breakfast. I pulled on bamboo slippers and opened the door to a crowd of Lesaries heading for the cafeteria. Rather than joining the Lesaries in a march to break down Moon City's walls, I fell into step with feet shuffling against ceramic tile. The people grinned widely and bowed their heads at me.

I smiled back. "Good morning."

They nodded again.

Inside the cafeteria, circular tables scattered about with wooden folding chairs at each one. Dad sat at one table with a young woman and man. At another table, Carper leaned forward talking with Jehoshua and Cherry, his expression fervent. Henry was nowhere in sight.

As I neared the empty seat next to Dad, people around the entire room began to stand at attention. I froze, noticing how their gazes followed me. Dad stayed put, wearing a look of confusion that I'm sure mirrored my own. Carper stood last, bowing before me and rising with a wink.

I struggled for words. It was just *me*. Pero the ordinary. Just because they depended on me to rescue them, didn't mean I was some queen.

"Um." I wrung my hands. "You may sit."

They obeyed but watched my every move. I sat at my spot, and still they waited. I motioned my head to the food in the center of the table. "Eat, please."

They turned their heads, picked up their bowls, and slurped. It seemed they'd roll over and play dead if I asked them to. I didn't get it. Too weird. This sudden devotion would take some getting used to.

I waved to the young man and woman at our table, then leaned close to Dad's ear. "What was that about?"

"You're their hero." Dad dished me up a bowlful of rice and watery broth.

As I took it from his hands and set it on the table, a chicken foot floated to the other side of the bowl. Apparently it hadn't made it across the road. I'd had camel and rabbit in the last few weeks but had dreamed of plain ole' chicken. Well, here it was, toe-nails and all.

"It's actually quite tasty." With his chopsticks, Dad plucked the foot from his bowl perfectly, like he'd been practicing his whole life. Friday take-out from Ping's didn't count. He yanked on one of the toes with his teeth, then chewed.

Back in Moon City, Mom avoided the meat. Traditionally, it hadn't been considered clean for Lesaries. Maybe I could be like Mom—a full-hearted vegetarian.

I picked up a white plastic soup spoon and slurped the broth. It was perfectly salted and carried the pleasing aroma of celery and thyme. "Any word on where Mom might be?"

"Jehoshua filled me in some," Dad said. "Sounds like whether these people find a safe place to go all depends on you finding your mom."

"No pressure. What else did Jehoshua say?"

"Before they were locked in, the Lesaries used this place as their sanctuary for many years. They gathered here and could go in and out of the walls freely. But when your mother—who was Carper's experiment because of her gift—found a portal and ran away from here at nineteen years old, everything changed for the Lesaries. During one of their meetings in this same spot, the walls closed permanently. They have been confined underground since then."

My eyes widened. "Trapped here since Mom was nineteen?"

Dad nodded. "That's why many parts of the Forbidden City are closed to tourists. The history books say the curators didn't allow access because the palace was so big, people would get lost or hurt, but now I know the real reason. No one is able to get in...or out."

"How did *we* get in?" Then I remembered. Carper used the key. "The necklace! Can't we use it to get out of the pagoda and to wherever Mom is?"

"The Lesaries are afraid because the guards are all around, threatening to lock them up if they ever attempt to escape. As if this isn't prison already. They are not allowed to worship Elohim here, but they do anyway."

What fear! To be caged in one place for decades was one thing, but knowing they will never really be free if they did escape was too much.

Dad took a sip of water, then set it back down. "You and your necklace are the key, but how to get out of here unnoticed is up to God Himself, I suppose."

I nodded. "I've seen Elohim's power before. He will make a way."

"I believe, Pero, but what if the miracle doesn't happen? What if *we're* stuck here forever?"

"There's a way." I nodded, assuring myself. "I wouldn't have come here with my necklace as a key if we were at a dead end."

The woman across from me picked up my bowl and scooped more broth. She placed it in front of me. "Eat."

"Oh." I nodded, then looked to Dad.

He smiled. "That's the only English word she seems to know. She's already given me two servings."

"Thank you." I smiled at the woman, wondering if another chicken foot was about to surface.

She beamed.

I finished the rest of my soup in silence, and the woman filled it up again.

"In China, some follow the custom of leaving your bowl full if you're done," Dad said. "Finishing your dish means you want more."

"Why didn't you tell me that before?"

Dad smiled. "Because if you lose any more pounds, you'll disappear."

I observed my stomach, flatter than it'd been a couple weeks prior. Must've been from my time in Moon City. "Do I look that bad?"

"Never." From behind me, Henry leaned down until his mouth grazed my ear and whispered. "You look beautiful this morning."

I sipped a drink of tea to dismiss the blush. He had to be kidding. I hadn't showered and my hair was a mess. Maybe I should go without a brush more often.

Dad scooted over to the next empty seat and patted the one he'd left. "Sit right here, Henry."

I shook my head. "That's not necessary."

"Sure, it is." Henry sighed and settled in his chair.

The woman handed him a bowl of soup.

Henry's eyes grew wide. "Yum." He spoke to the woman in Mandarin.

The woman replied.

I dropped my spoon. "You speak Chinese?"

Henry shrugged. "Uh, Carper taught me."

"Liar."

Henry smiled. "Liar that Carper taught me or liar that I told this lady that the food looks delicious?"

"Both."

He picked up the bowl and slurped. "Come on, Ro girl. This is good food. Maybe they'll have rabbit for lunch."

"My favorite." I rolled my eyes.

"So, what's the plan today?" Dad asked.

"Use Carper's money to buy peanut butter and Oreos," I said.

Henry scoffed. "How can you not like this? It's a staple."

"Pero's always been a picky eater," Dad said.

"Sorry." I tilted my head. Carper *did* have plenty of money to spare. "Actually, that may be a good idea. Not the Oreo part, unless you happen to be in a store and find some and you think of me."

Henry slurped on, and Dad took another bite from the chicken's pinky toe. Huh. No cookies for me.

I continued. "I'm sure the people here would like something nicer for a change after being stuck inside the Forbidden City for twenty-something years. Jehoshua said they've had an outsider sneak food in for them through a window, but it's been meager. Maybe we could somehow find food for them. We got in okay, so we should be able to get out, I think. And the guards aren't looking for us."

How had the Lesaries survived here for so long? The Chinese Emperor made sure there were plenty of rooms hundreds of years prior. But how did they carry on their lineage? Slim pickings and hopefully not involving relatives.

What was Sam—who was very much *not* my brother— doing at that exact moment? He probably started a garden and watched plants shoot up and blossom in minutes with his gift of growing. Strange gift. Cool, but seemingly useless. What did Sam think of the vision? Maybe he knew who the other woman's voice was. If only I could travel between portals and ask if—

"Pero?" Dad waved a hand in front of my face.

I jolted. "Yes?"

"We lost you there. I said that I liked your idea about finding supplies for the Lesaries, and then I asked if we should scout the land from the pagoda."

"Oh, right. Good plan. We might find a hint of where Mom is if we look for clues from the pattern Carper talked about."

"Right." Dad nodded. "The center. The *qí*."

Henry held up a finger for us to wait for him to swallow his food. "It would make sense that Elohim would choose the center of a maze to hide Bahar. Traditionally, Elohim's presence resides inside a curtain, where only the priests can enter, or in this case Elohim's chosen. Seems like having Elohim's power in the center of the emperor's gods would show His sovereignty as the beginning of all."

The Chinese woman and man across from us stood and bowed their heads.

"*Xiè xie*," the man said.

"*Zàijiàn*." Henry bowed his head.

While holding onto the man for support, the woman walked away, a visible limp in her step. They couldn't have adequate medical attention or supplies. These people needed help, yet Jehoshua said they could be persecuted once they left. If there was only a way to help them escape without the government noticing.

Carper approached our table and sat next to Dad. "I have a plan."

"Good morning to you, too," I said.

Carper waived his hand dismissively. "No need to observe the time of day and the mood it's in. Now, to the point. Pero, you join me and Jehoshua to scout the land from the top of the pagoda. We need to look for clues to the puzzle. Henry and

Matthew, you check the walls inside the palace. There's a door that leads from the sanctuary to the halls of the Forbidden City. With the key, we can get through, and Jehoshua knows when the guards are not on the lookout. After twenty years of being locked in, no one suspects anything. Knock on walls for any echo, look in spare rooms. See if there's a way out of here. But don't get caught."

"Couldn't we leave here from the wall that we came in?" I asked. "The one in the pagoda."

"Can't," Carper said. "I've tried it. Only works going in. But the door to the inside of the city works with the key."

But *I* hadn't tried the door to outside in the pagoda, and when we came in, there were no guards along that wall. It could work to go out that way, even if it had to be one person at a time. I rubbed the pendant between two fingers. I *was* a chosen. Had I been given the power to unlock it?

"Why don't *you* scout the inner city?" Henry asked Carper. "Since you know it so well."

Carper shook his head. "If they see me, it's over. Needs to be someone they don't know, such as lost tourists like you."

Henry stuck out his thumb and pointed at Dad. "Does Matthew look like the type to get lost? He's really good at puzzles too."

"Good point. Pero will go with you instead. Besides, it will look better to have a young couple so in love that they don't know which direction to go."

I rolled my eyes. "I'll go, but not because of what you said."

I felt Henry's quick turn toward me. "What does that mean?"

I shook my head. "I don't know. Never mind." What did I mean? That we weren't an item? Because we so were. I swiveled to Carper. "I have an idea, Carper."

"What's that?"

"We should buy food outside of the city if it's not too risky.

The Lesaries have been living off of hardly anything far too long."

"Agreed," Carper said. "With what money?"

"Really now. Can't you spare a little?"

"I would, darling, but I don't have a little."

"What do you mean? You're rich."

"*Was*, Pero. Until Elohim decided to humble me by taking it all away."

"But the plane tickets," Henry said.

"Free miles from years of traveling while living in this universe."

"And the *yuán* we got when we arrived?" Henry asked.

Carper grimaced. "Borrowed from Rose's stash in his underwear drawer. I would've never hired him back in the day if I'd known he hid money in such an obvious spot."

I held back a laugh. It was terrible, really. "What about the money you paid Rose?"

Carper rubbed his head. "May or may not have been from the Chinese government grant for my lab experiments." He paused. "Which is now depleted."

I didn't want to know how much he'd spent to experiment on Mom.

"You stole from the Chinese government." Dad shook his head.

"I didn't say that."

The sound of a guitar floated into the room followed by an explosion of singing. The room had emptied except for us. All bowls and food had been cleared from tables.

Jehoshua entered the room and stepped closer. "Come. Join us to worship Elohim."

We followed.

"For many years," he said as we walked beside him, "we didn't worship out loud, just in case they heard us and took our sanctuary. Now we hide from the outside, but we never hide our song."

Back home, I could attend a sanctuary whenever or wherever I wanted to worship Elohim, but I hadn't known what it meant. When I was with the Lesaries in Moon City, I'd experienced a different kind of faith than I'd known in Green Meadow. There was no fear to shout and circle around a city. No fear to celebrate Elohim's power, whether with the blast of a trumpet or the silence of our march.

These Lesaries hid. Yet they didn't sing to get out; they sang to praise the One who could.

Do not worry about tomorrow. Strength.

I had faith we'd find Mom. I had strength that I could do it. But if our plans fell apart and death threatened to shut my mouth, would I still sing?

12

移动

The doorknob's key hole was horizontal and flat, a seemingly perfect fit for, say, a wooden pendant in the shape of a feather.

I hovered my pendant over the key hole inside the sanctuary. Henry and I were assigned to explore the tunnel and search for Mom. "What if someone is waiting behind this door?"

Henry shrugged. "If it's a guard, I'll slug him. If it's your mom, I'll give her a big hug and tell her how much you missed her. Then maybe I'll let you hug her next."

"It's not funny, Henry. I'm scared to death right now."

He placed his hand on my shoulder. "At breakfast this morning, you were ready to kick some Botox."

I raised an eyebrow. "Did you mean to say buttocks?"

"Right, just what I said."

I grinned.

"Ah, there's that smile." Henry winked. "Ro, open the door."

I squared my shoulders and let out a breath. He sounded like some game show host where I'd either open a vault holding a fortune or a penny. Couldn't we settle for something in the middle? Something normal, for once, without the suspense that the wrong choice would put me behind bars? "Ready."

I opened the door, and the sound of it scraping along the floor was like a high-pitched laugh. My body trembled, eyes searching the darkness, then gradually adjusting. Nothing but an empty hall, appearing endless. Was Mom in there? It couldn't be that simple. What might hide under the basement of a city? Perhaps embers or giant, fire-breathing snakes. "I don't want to go."

Henry clicked on a flashlight. "I'm right next to you." He moved forward, and I forced myself to match his pace. The light illuminated each next step. Our heavy breathing and drips of water from the ceiling echoed against the brick walls and cement floor. The moldy smell made me want to sneeze, and the damp air brought a chill.

"Feel along the wall as you move," Henry said. "Look for any loose brick. It could be a hidden door."

"You think the emperors had that many secrets to keep?"

"Not sure, but there is one brick that I'm looking for." Henry moved the flashlight to the left and right, smacking the bricks with the bottom of his clenched fist. "My parents kept it hidden here."

"Your parents were in this exact tunnel?"

"I'm pretty sure this is the one. We helped the sanctuary here for a year. China was one of the many places Elohim directed my parents to. Mostly we brought in food and supplies. Though I've never been inside the sanctuary. Without the key to get in, we were limited to passing food through the small windows. My dad found access to this hall from the Forbidden City, and he hid money in one of the bricks in case of emergency."

"Why didn't you tell me about this when I had the idea of getting food for the Lesaries yesterday?"

"I didn't want to announce it in front of everyone, in case

the stash got into the wrong hands. That's why I wanted to go with you in this tunnel, though."

"It wasn't because we're charmed tourists who got lost in the haze of love?"

Henry bumped me gently. "That might've been part of it." Perhaps I imagined it, but I thought I saw him blush in the dim glare of the flashlight.

"How old were you when you helped your parents here?"

"Sixteen. My sister was fourteen."

"Only two years ago." I shook my head. "You've had more life experience in the last two years than I've had my whole life."

"Not true, Ro. You've had a lot happen in the last month."

"Being kidnapped doesn't count."

"Well, I can tell you one thing. Traveling around the world isn't as grand as you'd think. I don't know how to stay still."

"I don't think living in one place would calm you down, Henry."

"Could be true."

Henry's light shone on an object in the middle of the hall, which widened enough to walk around it.

"What's that?"

The flashlight beam revealed a statue of a Chinese warrior with stoic features, standing at attention.

I yelped, my heart thumping.

"Now I remember." Henry approached the warrior and turned left. "What we need is near the statue."

He walked to the wall and knelt in front of a red, clay brick with crumbling mortar. "Can you hold the flashlight for me?"

I moved slowly so I wouldn't trip in the dark, took the light, and aimed it at the wall. Henry loosened dirt from the edges, then wiggled it back and forth until it slid out, and he had the whole brick in his hands. A spider half the size of my hand scurried out, and I screamed. Henry picked the critter up by one of its legs and flung it away.

"That is so creepy."

"It's more scared of you than you are of it."

"You sound like my dad when you say that."

Without a glance in my direction, Henry reached into the space, wiped off cobwebs and dust, and lifted a Ziplock bag with a wad of money inside. He opened the bag, took out a handful, and placed the bag and brick back into place.

"This should be enough." Henry stood. "Now to the door out of here, which I believe is right past this statue."

"Finally." I let Henry pull my hand and guide me around the soldier whose large, vacant eyes seemed to follow me. "His serious face is creeping me out."

"Just wait till midnight when he starts to move."

"Funny, Henry."

"I never joke, Ro girl. I'm much too serious for that."

"So am I."

In a matter of seconds, the light flickered, dimmed, then shut off completely.

"Dang it." I heard Henry shake the flashlight and repeatedly click the switch.

"Great. You, me, and a grouchy statue in the dark with no way out."

"Would've sounded romantic if you left out the statue part."

"Oh, I'm very aware he's there, probably staring us down right now." I shivered. "Now what?"

"In this darkness, there's no way I'll find the door leading out of here. Guess we're going back."

"Fine with me. I've had enough spooky places for one day."

Henry let go. "This way."

I leaped forward, found his hand, and squeezed it tight. "Hey. You're stuck with me holding on the whole way back."

"Best news I've heard in a long time." Henry interlaced his fingers with mine and whistled a tune.

"Seriously?"

"Is there a problem?"

"You really want to bring up that song?"

"I'd rather have Legos get stuck inside my head than *Backstreet Boys*."

"Tell me why?"

He chuckled, lifted my hand, and kissed it. "I sorta like you, Ro girl."

I smiled in the dark.

13

———————

揭示

I awoke groggy and disoriented. What time was it? In my room, the clock on the wall said four in the afternoon. I'd slept for three hours? Walking through the tunnel with Henry must've wiped me out. Now I'd be up half the night.

I yawned, sat up, and put on the house slippers. Henry and I had agreed to check out the tunnel again tomorrow. He said the door next to the statue led to part of the Forbidden City open to tourists. It didn't seem like the best exit for the Lesaries since it would most likely open to an army of guards. Maybe Henry would go with me later tonight and check out the door leading out of the city and onto the street. Jehoshua said that exit didn't work, but I had the necklace.

After pulling through the knots in my hair with a comb Cherry had found for me, I headed out. I walked down the empty hall, then paused when I heard voices coming from one of the bedroom doors left slightly ajar. Cherry and Jehoshua. That was my cue to leave. They hadn't seen each other in years, Cherry had left Jehoshua behind, and they had issues to work out in their marriage that I didn't want to know about.

"I couldn't get into the sanctuary," Cherry said.

On second thought, maybe I'd listen for a minute.

"How'd you leave in the first place?" Jehoshua asked.

"Calvin gave me Bahar's necklace through the window, said that I could use it to leave through the tunnel and that he wanted to talk with me. He was sorry for being an absent father and wanted to make it up to me. I believed him."

Jehoshua's sigh was heavy. "Why didn't you tell me? We could've talked it through, made a plan in case something went wrong."

I heard Cherry's soft cry. "I knew you'd say not to go, that I couldn't trust my father. You would've been right. I wanted to fix things on my own, but it was a trap. Rose was in the tunnel and offered a large amount of money if I agreed to work for him. He said he'd give it to the sanctuary. We needed the money, and Carper knew that. I said 'yes' so that the Lesaries would live. Years later, I found out that none of the money went to us. It all went to Calvin and his experiments. I didn't trust in Elohim to provide and tried to make a way on my own, and it destroyed us."

"Love knows no bounds."

"I've messed up too much."

"You are not your father's; you are a daughter of the King."

I took a couple steps back to leave.

"I worry about Pero," Cherry said.

I froze. Stepping closer, I pressed my ear to the opening.

"She trusts Calvin completely. Says he's changed. But I don't think there's been enough time for him to prove himself. He's moody. One minute he pretends to be your best friend and the next he's aiming a gun at your head."

"I've wondered the same," Jehoshua said. "I want to believe he intends the best, but we need to be on high alert. Let me know if he starts talking about not having enough money or if he's emotional at all."

At breakfast, Carper mentioned he was out of money, but was that because I brought it up? Or was he really lying?

"What do you think about Pero being the chosen?" Cherry asked. "Is it true?"

"I sensed it the moment I met her. She's the one we've been waiting for."

I was the one to release Mom so that the sanctuary could unlock, and they could leave. If only Elohim would've directed me here sooner, but would I have accepted the call? My whole purpose in Moon City turned out to be rescuing Carper, which may not have been the best idea. Now that I was here again for Mom, I felt more ready, like I could handle more than I could've before my journey.

"Henry's a good guy," Cherry said. "They're a cute couple."

Guilt hit me in the gut. I needed to leave.

"And young. I don't think Pero's aware of the other part of the prophecy though."

My mouth fell open. What other part?

The click of a door startled me. I turned around to find Dad coming out of a room.

"Finally awake?" Dad drew closer, and I met him quickly so Cherry and Jehoshua wouldn't see me near their door.

"Just woke up." Minus a five-minute distraction in the hall. "I was on my way to find you, actually."

"Good timing. Jehoshua let me use their computer to research the Forbidden City."

"You're a walking history lesson. Why did you even need to research?"

Dad laughed. "Your old man doesn't know everything. I was specifically looking for meanings behind labyrinths."

"Trying to break the maze code?"

"I think I did." Dad started walking, and I followed. "In Greek Mythology—"

"Pero." Jehoshua stepped into the hall. "Can I talk with you for a minute?"

Uh-oh. My neck stiffened. He'd caught me spying.

"Is everything okay?" Dad asked.

"Everything's fine. Cherry and I want to check in with Pero. You're welcome to come too if Pero doesn't mind."

"I'll let you three talk. I trust her." He gave me a quick hug. "Meet me at the pagoda?"

"Sure thing."

Dad waved at Jehoshua, then walked away.

Cherry emerged from the room. "Hi, Pero. Did you have a nice nap?"

"I slept way too long."

"You probably needed it."

Jehoshua opened the door to the room Dad had left. "Let's chat in the office where there's better lighting."

We followed him into another small room with a desk, clunky computer that looked like it came from the early 2000's, and four folded chairs that Jehoshua opened and set out. Where the wall met the ceiling, light from a window poured in. I guessed this was the famous window where the Lesaries took supplies from Henry's family. Too small to squeeze through, but large enough to bring in food.

The chair squeaked as I sat.

Jehoshua arranged his seat so that he faced me and Cherry. There was no getting out of this one.

Jehoshua smiled, his bushy beard lifting in response. "Cherry and I wanted—"

I held up a finger. "Before you start, I want to say I'm sorry."

"For what?" Cherry asked.

"Uh." So, they didn't know. "For telling everyone to sit at breakfast this morning. It was kind of bossy of me, but I felt awkward and—"

"Pero, you're not in trouble." Jehoshua's beard stayed put as if firmly agreeing.

"Oh."

"Anything else you want to tell me?"

I scratched my head. "Well, uh...I may have heard you two talking...a little."

"I see." Jehoshua's expression never changed. "So, you must know why we want to check in with you."

"I have an idea."

Jehoshua nodded. "I want to hear from you on how you're doing, but before we start, let's pray."

I bowed my head and closed my eyes as I'd seen Lesaries do in Green Meadow's sanctuary back home. After a moment of silence, I opened my eyes and noticed Jehoshua held out his hands and lifted his face upward as if looking to Elohim's throne rather than down to his heart.

"Yahweh, your works are great. I see them in your people and in your faithfulness to us. Thank you for bringing my wife and Pero, your chosen and precious girl, home. Light the way. So be it."

"So be it," Cherry echoed.

Jehoshua and his beard smiled again. "Now, how is Pero Moshe?"

"Good."

"I'm glad. I'd love to hear more."

He reminded me of Shea: caring, patient. Maybe I should start calling him Shua. Shea and Shua. I held back a laugh and focused on a beetle on the ceiling. "How am I?" I looked back at him. "Honestly, I don't know."

"What do you mean you don't know?"

He would've made a great therapist. Where should I start? "I was kidnapped by Carper, assigned to rescue my mom, then told to save Carper instead. I've traveled between two worlds. My emotions are torn between two very different guys. Nightmares about my mom disappearing are gone, but now I'm hearing voices. The Lesaries here expect me to save the day. And just when I thought it couldn't get any worse, they served chicken feet for breakfast. I hate chicken feet."

Cherry smirked.

"I must not be a hero because real heroes eat chicken feet. Don't quote me on that."

Jehoshua laughed. "Tonight's dinner is chicken *legs*, so you should be okay." His smile faded. "Want to know what I think?"

I nodded, not wanting to seem nervous.

"You've been running away a long time, and it's Elohim's turn to lead you."

"I *have* let Him lead me. That's how I ended up here."

Jehoshua leaned forward, elbows resting on his legs and his fingers interlaced. "Are there areas in your life where you're still running away?"

"Not that I know of."

"You mentioned you're torn between two different guys. How does that make you feel?"

I was right. He'd make an excellent therapist. "Confused. One minute, I think I belong with Henry, but then I see Sam or hear his voice and I'm still drawn to him. It's like I'm running between two decisions and can't..." His point became clear, my mind spinning at my contradicting words. "Oh."

Jehoshua laid back against his chair. "You're home, Pero. No need to go anywhere."

"Then how do I make decisions?"

"There are times when you need to choose and believe it's right. I can't decide for you. But sometimes neither is the right choice, or it's the wrong timing. The next right step should be obvious. That doesn't mean you never will be stressed or indecisive when needing to make a decision, but I think you can tell the difference."

I could, which was why I should talk with Henry, tell him I

needed space for now. Sounded simple as long as my emotions weren't involved, which they would be.

"There's one thing you mentioned when I overheard you talking." I swallowed. "Something about me not knowing the whole prophecy."

Jehoshua closed his eyes briefly as if in prayer. "It's not time for you to know. It would confuse you more, bring you to conclusions before you've had distance from your situation."

"My relationship situation?"

"Yes."

Now I really wanted to know, but I trusted Shua's—I mean Jehoshua's—judgement.

"Any other questions?" Cherry asked.

"Yeah. How do I rescue the Lesaries?"

Jehoshua placed a finger on his chin. "I think the better question is, how does Elohim want to *use* you to rescue the Lesaries?"

"Do you have the answer?"

He shook his head and smiled. "Not yet, but we can trust that He will show the way."

Cherry looked at Jehoshua. "In so many ways, He already has." Her focus shifted to me. "I'm sorry for being rude when I first met you. Now that I'm home, I want to practice more kindness. Don't hesitate to let us help."

I nodded. "Thank you both. I feel loved."

You are, Elohim said, and I believed Him.

"One more thing," Jehoshua said. "Keep an ear and eye on Carper."

I nodded. "Will do."

14

———————

探索

Dad was in the middle of giving Henry and Carper another history lesson when I entered the pagoda. They looked out the window as Dad pointed down below.

"You see, the white spaces are maps for the same structure underground in the tunnels. The middle is where Bahar will be."

Henry flashed me a smile and shrugged.

"But you don't know that," Carper said.

"Not for certain, but it makes the most sense that Elohim would keep her safe in the middle of walls. His strength—His *koach*—protects."

"Such faith, Dad." I walked to the open window and leaned on the banister to take in the view. "The white spaces still look like lines to me."

"Macro before micro, Pero. Big picture first." He tucked me into a side hug and leaned close to my ear. "How was your talk?"

"Fine," I whispered back.

"Good." He turned back to the view below. "Mazes and labyrinths are different."

I smiled at Henry and shook my head, letting Dad's lecture fade into the background. Maybe Dad's theory was right. He did have a big heart behind that high IQ and was far more relaxed since leaving for China, as if his fear completely vanished at the hope of finding Mom. I didn't want him too disappointed if Henry's and my second exploration in the tunnels proved him wrong.

That'd be a good time to talk with Henry. I kinda-did, kinda-didn't want to stop our relationship, which was enough confirmation that I should probably pause. Wasn't easy though. It'd be another loss. Or would it? Maybe I could finally process where I'd been and where I was going. After all, boyfriends mushed brain cells.

Carper breathed out a dirty word. "Rose is down there."

"Where?" Henry asked.

Carper pointed at a patch of greenery, to the right of the maze. Between two rows of hedges, Mr. Rose paced.

"I never thought he'd come," Carper said. "He got his money. What else does he need?"

Jehoshua's warning blared in my head like a siren. Carper mentioned money again. But he was talking about Rose. Was that a concern?

"How do we get into the city without Rose noticing?" I asked.

Carper folded his arms. "That is a problem. He knows about the tunnels and will have them blocked. You didn't see anyone in there, right?"

"Only a creepy statue." I took in the steps that wound down from the steeple and to the entrance. "Can I *try* to find a way to use my necklace at the entrance door? I might be able to get out."

Carper sighed. "You haven't stopped bringing it up either.

We all know it only works from the outside. Henry, take Pero down there to check it out so she can get the idea out of her mind."

"No prob." Henry bolted from the lookout, grabbed my hand, and headed down the stairs. "Let's do this."

"What's the hurry?" I pulled my hand from his grip and ignored his confused look. I couldn't be holding hands with the guy I'd need to break up with.

Henry waited until we were halfway down, then whispered in my ear. "Carper's driving me crazy. He still thinks he's in charge of everyone and their pet eagle."

"You're right about that." I stopped walking and lowered my voice, failing miserably to keep space between us. "I overheard Jehoshua and Cherry. They said to be alert for any odd behavior from Carper. They don't trust him."

"Not sure if I do either. Listen to this." Henry put his arm around me and whispered. So much for keeping distance. "When I was coming into the pagoda, Carper was alone and on the phone. He saw me and automatically switched to Chinese. He doesn't know I understand Mandarin. Some of it was lost in translation, but one part I got clearly."

"What did he say?"

"'I need the money.'"

My heart skipped a beat. "That's not good. Jehoshua told Cherry to let him know if Carper mentioned anything about money. Apparently, that's been his downfall in history."

"Not his only downfall."

Too true. Had I assumed that Elohim's work in Carper would be permanent? That he'd never fail us again?

We continued walking down the stairs, reached the bottom, and approached the wall where I'd entered.

I touched the scratchy brick surface. "There's no frame for a door."

"That's because you were teleported in. No door needed for that."

"How'd *you* get in without a key?"

Henry hesitated. "My family...we're transporters."

I blinked. "You're what?"

"Transporters is a term that the Lesaries gave my family. We kind of appear places, and then Elohim directs us on what to do next."

"Whoa." And I thought visions were cool. "That's how you appeared at my house in Green Meadow."

"And how my family are world travelers."

"Were you all born that way?"

"Yes, and it's passed down from the prophet, Elias. That's why transporters marry other transporters. Otherwise, family life is hard if they don't all have the gift."

"I'm not a transporter." I pursed my lips. Did I have to point that out? A long future together might be difficult for us if he was always pulled away, unless I could somehow go with him.

Henry's face grew dim. "I know." He leaned against the brick wall, laying his head against it. A second later, he jumped away. "The wall moved!"

I studied where his head had laid. One brick had indented a quarter of an inch, and in the center was an engraved feather. "No way."

"Yes way." Henry stepped closer to the brick and picked up an object on the small shelf where the brick had moved in. "It's a car key."

"Interesting."

Henry put it in his short's pocket. "Maybe we'll find the car."

I pulled the necklace over my head and reached for Henry's hand. "In case we're teleported when I put the pendant in."

"Good plan." He squeezed my hand.

I should let go, but one last hold wouldn't hurt anything. Transition, right?

When I placed the feather into the engraving, it fit perfectly. The pendant glowed in blue light and made a soft buzzing noise.

"Something's working."

It continued to hum and light up, but nothing happened. Still holding onto Henry's hand, I reached for the pendant. "Maybe I need to touch—"

As soon as my finger touched the pendant, we were yanked back, then propelled forward like the start of a roller coaster ride. Lights flashed for a second, and we were standing by the brick wall from the outside of the Forbidden City.

"That actually worked!" I hopped and clapped my hands. "We can totally make this happen, Henry! And Rose will never notice the Lesaries escape from the sanctuary in a more secluded place like this."

I stopped when Henry didn't share my excitement.

"Where's your pendant?"

I felt along my neck, then gasped. "It's still in the key hole."

"Which means we can't get back in."

I dropped my head to my chest. "Maybe that's why Jehoshua said not to do it. I really need to get better at listening."

"But..." Henry placed his hand against his cheek and twisted his mouth. "The Lesaries will be able to get out that way if someone eventually notices that we're not back and checks downstairs."

"Brilliant!" I held out my fist, and Henry bumped it, his fingers exploding away like fireworks.

I tapped my fingers together. "Now we wait for someone to notice." I sighed. "Hopefully it doesn't take too long."

Henry held out a finger. "Or..." He pulled out the key from his pocket. "We find the vehicle for this and get lost."

"I am going to pretend I didn't hear such a terrible idea."

"Come on, Ro girl. Even if we don't find the vehicle, walking around the area sounds more fun than waiting for someone to let us back in."

"In case you don't remember, we're not in Green Meadow anymore."

"Right." He twirled the key around his finger. "You are in the company of someone who knows this area well and could take you back in less than an hour."

I rolled my eyes. "The Lesaries will look for us before we're back."

"What if they don't?" He raised his brows and cocked his head.

I grunted. "One hour."

"Yes!"

"No more than an hour, Henry Beggs. Do you hear me?"

He saluted me. "Yes, ma'am."

"I'm only agreeing because we should use this time to buy some food for the Lesaries. You still have the money from the tunnel, right?"

Henry tapped his right short's pocket. "Yep."

I held my arm out in the direction of the sidewalk ahead. "Then let's go look for a car. Or Oreos. Whichever comes first."

"How about a kiss for being so clever?"

Tapping the back of my hand to his pursed lips, I walked away. "Nice try."

He ran up to me and turned me around. "Wrong way."

"I knew that."

15

保持

I tucked my chin toward my chest as my eyes cast upward. "I'm not riding on a motorcycle."

"It's a scooter."

"Looks the same."

Henry pouted like a boy and dangled the key in front of me as if he really held a diamond ring. He glanced at the riding scooter, turned the handle-bars back and forth, and pressed the small wheels. "There's some air in there, I think."

"The pedals are rusted."

Henry studied them. "Not much."

"I suppose you want me to squeal like a girl while holding on tight to my knight in shining armor."

"You are a girl." He smiled.

"A girl who likes to walk."

"And fly on eagles."

He had a point. "Fine."

Henry dusted the seat off with his hand and had a seat. "Let's hope this thing works."

I rubbed my chin. "An abandoned scooter at the end of an alley? Doubtful."

He put the key in the ignition. "Here goes nothing." He turned the key, and the engine sputtered, then died. "Well, at least the key fits."

"Sounds broken. Too bad. Guess we'll be walking."

Henry tried again, and it moaned like a dying cow, then quit.

"I'm leaving!" I called out as I marched away from the end of the alley.

"Just one more try." Henry grunted, then hollered as it spurred to life with a loud, triumphant blast of the engine. Henry coughed when a cloud of grey smoke hovered around him.

I sighed, dragged my feet back to the scooter, and sat behind him, wrapping my arms around his torso. Saying a quick prayer, I tightened my grip.

"We haven't even left yet." He turned the handle which lunged the scooter forward.

To my annoyance, I let out a squeal. My hair waved in the wind. Henry weaved in and out of traffic. Cars honked. People on the sidewalks stopped and stared as the engine rattled us along.

I wished I'd worn a helmet. "Slow down!"

The reckless boy laughed. A few minutes later, Henry pulled up on a sidewalk and parked the scooter next to a cart full of slaughtered pigs hanging on wires, snouts facing the ground, skin ripped.

The butcher watched me, knife in hand, blood on his hands. "You buy."

I shook my head. Lesaries didn't eat pork. Although, after years of eating whatever people snuck through the walls, I doubted they'd complain.

Henry grabbed my hand, quickly passed a squatting boy with his pants down around his ankles and entered a two-story market that smelled like seaweed and spices. I took in bright florescent lights, people stopping to stare at us, an escalator moving up to what seemed to be more food, Chinese characters on brightly-colored packages, a happy pop song blaring through the speaker.

Henry picked up a purplish-red, leathery-like fruit with scaly spikes on the exterior. "Ever tried dragon fruit?"

"Nope."

Henry placed ten in his cart. "Let's load up on rice and beans so we don't use too much of the emergency fund."

"How are we going to carry all this back?"

Henry's eyes perused my legs. "You're a girl who likes to walk."

I jabbed him. "Such a gentleman."

At the end of the rice aisle, a mom pushed a cart with a toddler sitting in the seat. She pointed a chubby finger at me. "Ma." A hiccup followed.

I gave a little wave.

The mom turned around, took one look at me, and talked to her baby. I heard her say *American*. Was it that obvious?

The girl giggled and revealed tiny teeth. I froze. That smile. Her laughter. Memories slammed against my gut like a boxer's glove. I was smaller than that girl once. But when I was born, my eyes couldn't have sparkled like this girl's. I'd been left by my birth mom. Under a tree. Until Bahar found me and held me, only to let me go when I was three. I'd grown up before my small self could latch onto a mother's hand.

Why did they leave me?

Henry's hand joined mine. I squeezed his fingers. Desperate.

Where had I gone? Where was I going?

Purpose.

To find Mom. Because she'd found me as a baby and took me in.

To rescue the Lesaries. Because I'd found them waiting for someone to carry them home.

———

"What happened in there?"

I rubbed my arm and took a deep breath. Around me, men in black suits sat at round tables and shouted in Chinese while drinking an amber liquid from shot glasses. No music played over head, yet the unfamiliar language from their tongues sounded similar to the Chinese opera I'd heard playing from a nearby vendor selling sun umbrellas.

"Since I got here—" I didn't meet Henry's eyes and instead focused on the dumplings in a bowl in front of me. My stomach growled at the intoxicating smell, yet I couldn't get myself to eat. "I don't know. I've been thinking about where I came from. Being a baby under a tree, abandoned. Then hearing that lullaby last night..." I rubbed my temple. "The voice singing might be the woman who brought me into this world."

"Your birth mom?"

"No." I picked up the chopsticks and watched the dumpling slip from my grasp. "Bahar, the woman who left me."

One chopstick slipped from my hand and landed on Henry's plate. Henry covered my hand with his own.

I looked up and met the sweetest blue eyes. Caring. Probing.

My eyes swelled with tears and shifted to my plate.

"Pero."

His gentleness lifted my face to his.

"Don't ever..." He rubbed his thumb across my palm, sending shivers up my arm. "Never forget Who first chose you."

A tear dropped to my chin, and I dabbed it with my shoulder.

Henry reached across the table and wiped another tear

before it had a chance to leave. "The reason you were born is because He loved you first."

I nodded.

"Elohim loved you before your parents did. Before I did."

I let go of his grip and sat back.

Henry held up a hand. "You're not ready to say it. I understand. We're still figuring all this out."

I wiped the remaining tears from my eyes as the waiter brought a plate of duck, thin wraps, slices of onion, and a dark brown sauce. The aroma was the best I'd smelled so far.

"*Xiè xie*," Henry said, and the waiter left.

I let out a breath. "I'm sorry, Henry." I wanted to love him, but my emotions were too scattered. "I need to sort through how I feel about all this change over the last month. It's more real all of a sudden."

"I'm here if you want to talk."

I hung my head. "I think we should...take a break from this relationship. I'm so confused about us right now, but I also don't want you to leave. I feel safe around you." Somehow, dependence made me stronger.

"Let's think about it. But I'm still your bodyguard first. I'm not going anywhere."

I smiled and picked up the chopsticks from his plate. "Teach me?"

He showed me how to use the chopsticks to put the steaming duck and onion into the wrap and how to fold it without the contents spilling. With a hand cramp, I figured out how to pick up the wrap and dip it into a soy sauce. My hard work was rewarded at the first bite. Juicy, tender, salty flavor exploded against my tongue.

"This is the best dose of dopamine I've ever tasted." I chewed and swallowed, temporarily satisfied and ready for my next bite.

After the meal, Henry set both bags of groceries on the

metal racks on the sides of the scooter. Instead of riding, he pushed it while I walked along. "Have any ideas on where your mom might be?"

"My dad seems to think she's in the middle of the tunnels. I guess we could give it a try when we go explore again tomorrow." Wait. Mom was the only other person who had a necklace. "I just realized that if the Lesaries follow us out of here, then none of them can get back in. And then what are we going to do? Wait around outside the city until I find my mom?"

Henry stopped. "I should've thought of that. We can go through the tunnel right now to get back in. I remember another entrance. We'll have to go through the Forbidden City, and there's a chance we'll run into Rose."

Henry and I might be able to sneak through the city without being seen, but how would we walk eighty people through without eyes all over us? The fastest way I'd seen anyone escape was when they'd traveled to another world. "That's it! Instead of using the exit through the pagoda, we get everyone out through the tunnel and enter a portal to the other universe. There's got to be a way to open one. If we can find my mom, I'm sure we can find an opening."

"You may be right." Henry moved to the other side of the scooter. "But where is Bahar? What if she's not in the Forbidden City?"

"You mean like she escaped?"

Henry nodded.

"Impossible. The rest of the Lesaries would've known." Wouldn't they? "As soon as my mom escapes, the sanctuary's doors will open."

"Where would your mom have hidden if she's in the Forbidden City?"

I focused on the street, weaving around the pieces of trash on the ground. "A closet."

"You sound so sure."

"That's how she left before." I furrowed my brow. "And a tree."

"Wood."

"What?"

"Closets are made from wood, wood from trees. So, we look for openings inside. Doors. Windows."

"Walls," I said.

"What?"

"My mom hid behind walls once. It's one of the only things she told my dad from her past. She said, the less we knew the better."

Henry gave a low whistle. "There's a lot of walls in the palace."

"Yes, but what walls would trap her?"

"I have a feeling you know the answer."

I shook my head. "I don't, but I think it would be a house of some sort. Every house she's lived in has been a trap, even the one my dad and I lived in with her. She couldn't leave without fear that someone would find her."

"Are you sure there was never a place where she felt safe?"

Mom had been trapped in our home when I was little, in Carper's home, in a dead emperor's home. When she lived with the Lesaries, she traveled without a home until her first husband, Salmon died. *Wait.* Did she feel safe with Salmon? Sam had mentioned a home she'd lived in before. He'd said it was her only sanctuary. Perhaps Mom was in a safe place now.

"We should check any places that resemble a safe place to hide. Maybe a room, a big wall that stands out. Not ordinary. Something beautiful or peaceful."

Direct us, Elohim. Take us to your perfect garden.

After returning the scooter to the back of the alley, we carried the two bags of food to the secret entrance we'd teleported from. It remained closed, and I still had no key.

"What should we do with the food?" I asked.

Henry sighed. "We can try to bring it inside the Forbidden City and pass it through the window."

I nodded. "Let's do it, then."

With the bags of food in hand, we walked around the block and joined the mob of people entering Tiananmen square.

"Wow." I took in the vast courtyard, the white cement blaring against the sun. Thousands of people spread out and still there was empty space. In the center of the square was the famous picture of Mao. His chin protruded and his eyes focused ahead.

"This way." Henry led me to the end of Tiananmen square. I squinted against the bright rays of the afternoon sun. As we got closer to a wall separating the square and the Forbidden City, I noticed small bars at the base. A passerby would more than likely dismiss the small space as an entrance to a sewer. But it was clearly the window leading to the sanctuary's office.

Henry set the bags near the bars, then scanned around us. "I'm sure no one will notice us, but just in case, I'm going to crouch here, and you'll sit behind me. Take one food item at a time and slide it through the space. The tourists shouldn't pay attention, but watch out for guards. I'll let you know if I see one, and you pause."

"Got it," I whispered.

Henry got into a squatting position.

"How do you keep your feet flat and not fall over?"

"Practice." He took one more glance around. "Looks clear. You can start."

Body tingling, I sat at an angle behind Henry so that my right arm hid behind his back. Then I carefully picked up one item, gave a quick look out for guards, and slid the food through the bars. Thankfully, they were all small enough to fit, and about ten agonizing minutes later, I dropped the last package through.

With a big sigh, I stood and shook out my legs. Henry stood, picked up the empty bags, and crammed them into the nearest trashcan.

"I didn't hear anyone in the room," I said. "Should we try to let them know about the food?"

Henry shook his head. "Don't want to bring more attention to their existence. If China knew a certain group of the government was holding a whole group of people hostage, it would cause an uproar. We don't want to start a war when we're so close to escaping."

"Makes sense."

Henry dipped his hand to the ground near the window, then stood and led me away.

"Did you drop something?"

"No. It was a note letting the Lesaries know we can't get back in and we're heading to the tunnels."

"Clever."

Henry stayed quiet as we walked through an archway with bright red walls on both sides and hundreds of gold-painted knobs. He touched them on our way through. "It's good luck and will bring you boys."

I smirked. "As in baby boys?"

"Correct."

"You want boys, huh?"

"Someday. Why not?" He smiled as if his thoughts scheduled his future. "How about you?"

I let out a nervous laugh. "I don't know what I want."

When I said it out loud, I realized how true it was. I wanted to be in a relationship. Or not. I loved Henry. Sort of. But like Mom, I felt caged, waiting for someone to find the door to my future.

Henry led me through ponds with lilies and frogs, over quaint white bridges and past clay pots taller than me. I walked around a room where the emperor's throne sat vacant behind ropes that kept tourists away.

"Do you know where you're going?" I asked Henry who'd taken us to a large room where the emperor's wives had once been trapped. Perhaps they hadn't felt that way. Maybe life seemed to offer them the best that they knew. Sometimes it's better not to know the taste of freedom.

"I think it's near here." He scoured the premises as if a hidden door would appear underneath one of the hundreds of cots. Henry stepped closer.

A guard approached him. "No step behind rope."

Henry and the guard conversed in Mandarin, then Henry motioned for me to come. The guard left.

"He said the emperor's wives used to fill the cisterns with water." Henry pointed to the large pots outside of the building. "I think these are the ones that will get us to the tunnels. The guard gave us permission to climb into a pot for a special performance. Follow my lead."

Henry stopped in front of four large pots with painted blue flowers trailing across them. One had a crack starting from the top to the bottom in the shape of a lightning rod. Henry climbed in, ducked down, and popped back up. "Yep, this is the one." He held out his hand for me to follow.

"What are you doing?"

"Getting in the pot." Henry winked.

"You've lost it." I took his hand and climbed in. The pot reached my chest. "That woman's staring at us."

The woman's eyes lit up, and she held out her phone. "You celebrity?"

"Yes."

I leaned close to Henry. "You sure about this?"

The woman talked rapidly to the man near her, then back to Henry. "You David Copperfield."

"Yes."

I laughed. Henry put his arm around me, and a repeated click sounded from the woman's phone.

Henry said *thank you* to the woman who clapped her hands and left with her husband.

I folded my arms and turned to Henry. "Explain yourself."

"Diversion." Henry shrugged. "She left, so it must've worked."

I opened my mouth to respond, but the woman came back. With a crowd.

"Who is David Copperfield?" I asked.

"American magician who's adored in China." Henry grinned. "I look nothing like him."

"I suppose you're about to perform a magic trick to make us disappear."

Henry leaned close to my ear. "Believe, Ro girl."

I shoved down the flutter in my belly. Would he continually enter my heart for one beat and leave the next?

Many gathered and chatted in excitement, taking more pictures than if the emperor himself appeared from his grave.

Henry glanced at my neck. "I forgot that we need the feather pendant."

"I don't have it, remember?"

Henry rubbed his temple with his fingertips. "I'm unsure how to make this work without it."

"You better figure something out, or we'll end up being cooked in here. I'm guessing that if you put me in broth, I won't float to the other side."

Henry's intense gaze never wavered. "Pray."

"What am I praying for exactly?"

Henry muttered while smiling and waving at the crowd. "That the magic trick works without a feather pendant."

I tilted my head to the side.

"Ladies and gentlemen!" Henry shouted in an impressive theatrical voice. "On the count of three, watch me disappear with this beautiful woman."

Oh, brother.

Henry translated, then held up his fingers and counted to three. The crowd counted with him.

One.

What would we do? Tuck ourselves into the pot and pretend they couldn't find us, like we were three-year-olds playing hide-and-go seek?

Two.

I scanned the crowd, enthusiastic faces counting with my kid-at-heart boyfriend. One face didn't smile. I did a double-take, then gasped.

Mr. Rose stared back at me with a scowl.

Three.

Henry ducked down into the pot and pulled me down with him.

"Henry, I saw Rose. We won't make it out of here without—"

A click sounded from the bottom of the pot.

"Your prayer worked."

"But I didn't pray."

Henry met my eyes. "Ready for the ride of your life?"

The floor fell, throwing us down like we were being shoved into a trashcan with a push-in lid. My stomach flew to my throat. A tiny whimper escaped my lips as we dropped into the darkness.

16

跟随

Falling. Deeper and deeper down.

Falling like the walls in Moon City. Like my fear. Like my ability to discern which direction was which. Were my decisions right-side-up or upside-down?

We crashed into water with a giant splash. My body plunged. All sound absorbed. It was just me floating in a space between the speed of life. Stuck. Unmoving. Lungs burned, seeking the end to a slow-motioned pause under the water. What felt like an eternity later, my body rose, my hands up and aching for the light. I reached the surface, then gasped for air and kicked my legs back and forth. Henry reached out and pulled me onto the bank. I lifted my aching body and laid in the grass. Slime from dirty water clung to my skin. I breathed hard.

Henry sat next to me, panting. "That was a longer drop than I remember."

I lifted my head slightly and laid back down.

"You okay?" He wiped a piece of algae from my cheek.

"I think so." My head throbbed. Colors spun around me. I squinted my eyes shut.

"Don't black out on me."

I opened my eyes and blinked. The colors subsided. I sat up.

"Easy." Henry grabbed my hand. "Don't get up yet."

I glanced around to see sunlight streaming into a deserted bath house. A very deep bath apparently. Cracked marble pillars climbed to the sky above a wall of dirt. Birds fluttered in and out of tree tops. Patches of grass covered the dirt floor, and over-grown shrubs covered a round-stoned path that led to an archway and beyond that a dark hall. "Where are we?"

"Underground near the tunnels."

"How'd you..." I rubbed my head.

Henry sat beside me and crossed his legs as if to settle in to tell a story. "When my family lived here, my parents searched for a way to get to the sanctuary so they wouldn't have to send food through the window. Elohim told them to go through a pot. They were unsure if He really said that, of course, but they gave it a try. There are a lot of pots in the Forbidden City. It took months. They found the right one, but it needed a key. Cherry took the key from Carper who lived here at the time. Cherry wasn't yet a Lesarie. My parents finally got in, but instead of the pot leading to the sanctuary, it took them to another part of the underground city that had access to hidden rooms. My parents showed me and my siblings the entrance when we returned years later, just in case we needed access someday."

"I didn't realize this place was so big." I rubbed my temple.

"A lot of rooms are hidden from the public." Henry touched my head and examined. "No blood. How's it feeling?"

"Like I got hit with one of Dad's textbooks."

Henry grimaced. "Let me know if you start feeling sick." He touched my head again, but this time his thumb lingered at my brow before grazing down to my chin.

I let myself look at him then, and a million thoughts raced through me. I loved him. Those blue eyes! I loved him not. I should take a break. The timing wasn't right. Henry smiled.

Those lips! I'd come alive when he kissed me the first time. I wanted—no, I couldn't. Henry tilted my chin, his eyes traveling to my mouth. My head stopped throbbing and instead my heart responded.

It had to be right that I wanted him near.

Nearer.

As his lips met mine, we both pulled away in a flash with the lingering feeling of slime and taste of salt.

Henry spit on the ground.

I sat up and wiped my mouth with the back of my arm. The salty taste moved to my tongue.

"Ugh, it's worse!" I spit until a stream of saliva plopped on the ground. "What was in that water?"

Henry laughed so hard that the dimple on his cheek looked more like a crater.

"So not funny." My cheeks burned, yet I couldn't help but smile.

Henry rubbed his face with his hands. We locked onto each other's eyes.

He shook his head. "Ro, girl." He sighed.

"What are we—I mean." I dropped my gaze.

"I get it."

"I'm not sure if you do."

Henry squeezed out excess water from his shirt. I averted my eyes to the birds. Attraction was easy. The question about whether we should be together wasn't.

"If I'd been born in Green Meadow," Henry started, "and had gone to Green Meadow High, and we had met in, say choir..."

I grinned. It would've been neat to grow up with Henry.

"And say you'd grown up with your mom and dad around and we lived a normal life..."

I shook my head. "Doesn't sound like you to live a normal life."

"Doesn't sound like you, either."

"You're the adventurous one." I scratched at my arm. Gunk had gathered under my fingernails. "I've spent most of my life being afraid."

"I don't believe it. Why'd you go for a run to the edge of your driveway every day?"

"Because I needed to get out." Wanted something more.

"Like me, you have an adventurous spirit, which is why you and I can't figure this out."

I raised my brow. "What about at lunch today? You said you loved me."

"I do love you." His Adam's apple bobbed up and down from a hard swallow. "Which is why I agree with you. We need to take a break."

I sat up straighter. The shift brought a chill from my damp clothes. "I thought *I* was taking a break."

Henry nodded. "I don't want to be in a relationship that you're not sure about. We need time to think through this, until we figure out if two adventurous friends should be in a relation-ship or if they'll..."

"Kill each other?" I smiled.

"Hey, we've argued a lot less since I kissed you."

I laughed. "The first or second time?"

"Whatever just happened doesn't count." Henry stood, reached out his hand, and helped me to my feet.

I squirmed under his gaze. Picking up a wet leaf plastered against my shirt, I set it on Henry's shoulder. "There. Now a part of me will never *leaf* you."

PAST THE SLIMY and stagnate water, we entered a dark hall that smelled like mold and dirt. Roots hung from cracks in the ceiling as if the trees were fighting to take back their land.

Henry tugged on a long root and swept cob webs out of our way. The sunlight from the pool faded from view and left us in deeper darkness.

I latched onto Henry's arm to steady myself.

"Pat your hand against the wall to feel your way."

"And also feel spiders crawling." I shuddered. "No, thank you."

Something fluttered along the ground to my left. I yelped. "What was that?"

"A rat. We probably scared it with our smell."

"Oh, come on. We smell perfectly fine." I sniffed Henry's shoulder and gagged.

He chuckled.

"You've been through this dark, scary tunnel before?"

"Only once. With my family."

"Still." I swallowed. "Seems darker than the other tunnel we walked through. I think this place will give me nightmares for the rest of my life."

"So dramatic."

"Been hanging out with you too long." I squeezed Henry's arm. "What do we do about Rose?"

A gentle hum stopped me in my tracks. I listened, but only heard the drip of water and something lightly falling onto my head. Screeching, I brushed it off.

"What happened?" Henry asked.

"A dirt shower." I reached for his hand, found it and squeezed. "Let's keep going."

My clothes clung to my legs as I stepped forward, my feet heavy. I was glad to have worn the lightweight shorts and shirt a Lesarie woman had given me.

The hum returned, but this time louder.

"Do you hear that?"

Henry stopped. "Maybe another rat."

"That's not it."

The hum turned into a melody. The same lullaby I'd heard the previous night.

My child, I love you.

The words repeated as a refrain.
My child, I love you. My child, I love you.
The message beat into my head and moved its way down my body as if I were digesting the words for the first time.

Why should it matter where I was going? All I needed to know was Love.

"Ro, talk to me."

Henry had moved closer than I realized, yet I felt removed. Like this voice who sang to me was Elohim Himself and everything and everyone dimmed in His presence. But it wasn't Him. It was a woman's voice. Motherly. Perhaps *my* mother's.

Could finding Mom be as easy as following her song? I let truth sink into my ears and drip into my core. No matter how far the two worlds divided us, Mom's song would pick me up again and remind me: My child, you are loved.

"Ro?"

"Elohim wants us to follow the voice."

Henry squeezed my hand to let me know he listened.

"I think it's my mom's voice." I swallowed the lump in my throat. "She's calling me because she's always loved me."

The stagnant air held moisture from the dirt above. I breathed in the smell of soil so strong that it seemed I might suffocate. I began to see shapes, such as the length of the walls on both sides of us, the shadow of Henry, the occasional rat darting by. But my sense of hearing was what spurred me on.

"This way." I turned to the right, forgetting the spiders and using my hands against the wall to guide me.

"Does her voice sound closer?" Henry asked.

I nodded, then remembered that Henry couldn't see. "Yes."

I only led us the wrong way once. We'd had to backtrack, then turn toward what could've been another hall.

I heard the voice more clearly, but it was deeper than Mom's. Maybe it wasn't her voice I'd heard all this time.

I tripped at my next step and felt ahead of me. "Stairs."

"We must be near the end."

At the top of the steps, I made a left turn. Light ahead outlined a rectangular shape.

"Is that a door?" I asked.

"Possibly. Let's check it out."

When we drew closer, light illuminated the sides of the wall. Elaborate paintings covered the walls, floor to ceiling. The dim light revealed art of Chinese warriors on horses and gods bathed in gold.

"Woah," Henry said.

I touched the picture of a woman holding a child before an altar. "I wish Dad could see this. He'd probably know all about it."

"My parents never got this far." Henry gave a low whistle. "I wonder if anyone knows about this place"

I let Henry's comment go, focusing all my energy on the woman and child. Why did she bring her child to the altar? Perhaps it was a human sacrifice, or maybe she hoped for an answer for her child's safety or health. I wanted to believe the latter. A loving mother did anything to save her baby. But hadn't I been sacrificed before that loving mother came along? And didn't both my moms leave because they couldn't save me?

I shuddered. I refused to believe I was someone's garbage. Elohim treasured me, and so did Mom.

My child, I love you.

The words were sung louder, and I jumped at the voice's nearness. The light. She had to be behind the light.

As I reached for the wall, I placed my hand against a wooden door that lit up at my touch. I gasped and tried to pull away, but my hand wouldn't budge. The heat increased until unbearable in intensity.

I shouted, begging for the pain to stop. Fire pulsed through my arm and into my body until I felt like I'd been jolted by lightning.

I vaguely registered Henry trying to pull my hand free.

The singing grew loud as a roar.

Even in your suffering.

I ducked my head to muffle the sound. My body shook as the voice vibrated through my body.

Even in your pain.

The fire. The burn. Pulsing. Throbbing. Yes, I was in pain. Couldn't it stop? I cried so loudly that I thought all of the Forbidden City must hear.

Even in your discomfort.

No. I didn't want discomfort. I wanted to be a little girl with her mother, lulled to sleep, never having to know the pain of grief and trouble and persecution.

No to death! No to Lesaries needing to hide! No to Mom wasting all of our lives by running!

No, no, no.

I screamed for Mom, for the Lesaries, for the world and all of its groanings. I screamed until I emptied as much feeling as I could.

How long, Yeshua?

He was all I could think of, God in the form of a man who'd

come to give me rest. He'd wiped the dirt from my feet with His hands and came to my world to minister to me.

"How long will we suffer?" I shouted.

Just when I thought my skin would melt, a voice boomed in my head.

Stop!

Elohim's presence settled in the room. My pain vanished.

A whistle shrilled through the air, like the wind crying. The air grew colder, picking up until a gust threw my hand away from the lit wall, and then it stopped.

I wiped tears. The wall revealed a doorway, the light from the other side streaming through. But instead of looking forward, I peered to my right at the painting. The mother who'd held her child at an altar now held the child in her arms.

You are my daughter, Elohim said. *Beloved one.*

Elohim rescued me from the pain of myself. And He would again. I could trust Him.

Henry rested a hand on my arm. "You okay?"

I smiled at him and nodded, knowing this time he could see me through the light. Something sticky covered Henry's face, but it didn't matter.

With renewed confidence, I pushed the door open—Henry right behind—and took my first step.

17

学习

Stone gods dressed in gold lined up on an altar. Above, Chinese characters were written in gold against a black background. To the right of the altar hung a bright red curtain.

Large torches on either side of the altar lit up the room. I shook, even though the room was warm.

"You feel it too?" Henry asked.

"What?"

"There's some kind of spirit here. It's cold."

Maybe that's what I sensed, something unseen but at work. Unlike Elohim, it felt empty. Lonely even.

"Do you hear anything in here?" Henry whispered as if the cold spirit awaited and listened.

"Not the song." I strained to listen, and a slight hum echoed from someone's ritual chanting. "But we need to find a way out soon. I have a feeling this room still gets used."

Henry peeked behind the curtain. "Nothing here but a wooden wall."

He slid his hand against it. "You'd think Sam was in here,

with how smooth this wall is." He dropped the curtain. "Sorry to mention him. That was awkward."

"Doesn't need to be." It totally was. Needing a diversion, I lifted the curtain and touched the wall. At the touch, a slight current pulsed through me. I let go.

"There's nothing behind the curtain," Henry said.

I put my hand back onto it, and the same current traveled through it, but faster. Now that I was certain I could remove my hand, I kept it there.

Are you coming? Sam's voice spoke clearly as if he stood right beside me.

Mom's voice whispered through the wall. *Elohim, where do I go?*

I dropped my hand from the wall. "I felt some sort of power when I touched the wall. I think this is the entrance."

Henry hurried to my side and placed his own hand on the wall. "I don't feel anything. She must be calling for *you*."

I touched the wall again. The power I'd felt the first time doubled in intensity. It didn't hurt, but I felt my hand warm and energy leave me. The wall began to move like the ripple of a stone on water and became translucent until it took on the shape of an entryway. The entrance displayed a garden. Birds chirped from the opening and butterflies traveled past brightly-colored flowers.

I glanced over my shoulder. "You're seeing this, right?"

"Sure thing. You ready?"

I gulped. "What if I can't get back?"

"If Elohim can open doors to let you in, I'm sure He'll get you out."

I took a deep breath. "Henry?"

"I'm right here, Ro girl."

I took a deep breath. "You're so good to me."

"Go," he whispered.

A rumbling noise gave me pause. "There aren't eagles here, right?" The distant roar reminded me of their flapping wings.

"I hear it too." Henry scanned the room. "You should get out of here while you have—"

The sound of a bell resounded, increasing in volume until both of us covered our ears. No bell would have the ability to ring that loudly unless it was special. My pulse picked up speed.

"Someone must've rung the bell in the pagoda!" I shouted.

"What?"

Behind Henry, a bright fog swept through the crack of the door we'd just walked through, then it traveled through a hall. "Is that gold?"

"It's gold fog!" Henry yelled near my ear.

"That's what I just said."

"What?"

Someone had to have rung the bell. Was it Carper?

"You need to leave!" Henry yelled.

"So do you!"

The gods on the altar began to tremble, as if they, too, would come alive. Then, they did. Their eyes turned gold and as bright as stars; their mouths a bloody red.

I screamed.

Henry brought me close, and I hid my face in his chest.

"Go now, Ro!"

"I won't leave without you!"

The door we'd come through banged open. I screamed again.

Stone soldiers marched in a line, the one from the first tunnel taking the lead.

Gold fog surrounded us, until I could no longer see.

Henry pushed me forward, lifted the curtain, and hid us behind it. The fog began to pour in beneath the curtain. Henry took my hand and placed it on the wall. It began to warm.

"No," I yelled. "I can't lose you again."

He leaned in close. "Goodbye's not forever for us."

Henry let go.

My body moved through the wall, and the room started to fade. With a flash of motion, a figure charged Henry from behind.

"Watch out!"

A guard yanked him away.

The curtain fell, and the wall closed behind me. The chaotic noise of the bell and the commotion from statues and guards completely faded. I rested my head against the wall, the wood smooth against my forehead. What was that? Walking statues. Gold fog. Things like that didn't happen.

Taking a couple of deep breaths, I turned, then gasped. The sun warmed my neck. Perfect breeze. Not too hot, nor too cold. Red, purple, yellow, and orange flowers clustered around the bottom of red pine trees. Cicadas buzzed. The walls enclosed the garden, big enough to walk around, but small enough to see the premises.

I stepped into a gazebo and sat on a white bench. In a pond nearby, koi darted around each other, as if in a hurry to go nowhere.

Like me. No place to go inside a safe haven while Henry battled guys with guns and gods with bloody mouths.

Only one person for me to find here. But where was she? I'd expected Mom would be waiting for me with open arms and us figuring out the next plan together.

Yet I was alone. Or so it seemed.

At the stirring in the brush nearby, I scanned the bushes, the trees, the plethora of flowers. Someone peaked around a pillar and darted back behind when spotted. Even though she hid quickly, it seemed to be a young woman about my age with long black hair. She stepped out into the clearing, one hand secured on the pillar like she was ready to hide behind again if I showed any threat.

"Who are you?" she asked. "How'd you get in here?"

I stood slowly. "Pero Moshe. I'm looking for my mom. I was led here. Well, her voice led me here." Lovely. I'd just met this woman and told her that I heard and followed voices.

"I don't understand."

I rubbed my head. "Me neither." I held up my hands. "I won't hurt you. Promise. Maybe you can help me."

Her mouth twisted, and she cocked her head, examining me from head to foot. I must've looked desperate with mud streaked all over my body, hair, and clothes.

"You figured out how to enter, so could you get us out?"

"I was hoping my mom would know." I glanced at the bright blue sky. Mom wasn't up there. I didn't expect her to be, though. No over-sized eagles to fly on in this world.

I turned back to the woman. She'd taken a few steps forward. Although her words indicated she was leery of my intrusion, her body appeared relaxed. Her tan brightened deep brown eyes that seemed vaguely familiar. Delicate features fit her face perfectly. Thick waves of hair cascaded right above her hips. She wore a white cami and beige, loose-fitting pants. She was beautiful.

"Have you been here long?" I asked.

"No." She furrowed her brow. "I mean, I'm not sure. I had to get away from Dr. Carper. A big machine appeared over there." She pointed to a bush. "I went through it, I think." She shook her head, as if waking from a dream.

Her story sounded crazy as mine. "You know Dr. Carper?"

She did a double take. "Unfortunately."

"Some say he's dead, but he's very much alive and annoying as ever."

"There are many terrible words I could use to describe Dr. Carper. Annoying isn't one that comes to mind."

I studied her. "Did he hurt you?"

The woman halted. "Doesn't matter. I'm away from him now, if I can find a way out."

I stepped down from the gazebo. "What's your name?"

She stuffed her hands in her pant's pockets. "Bahar Abram."

I choked on saliva. "Excuse me?"

Her eyes widened. "You know me?"

One quick laugh burst out. Impossible. I plopped down on the final step. "Bahar Abram is my mom."

18

离开

I recognized the slim brows, the big brown eyes, the gorgeous black hair. The girl's face before me didn't hold as many wrinkles as Mom did then, her eyes didn't appear as fatigued. But her countenance appeared the same: calm, graceful, confident. Not at all like me.

"You're not making sense," she said. "I don't have a child, and if I did, she wouldn't be roughly the same age as me."

I exhaled, long and slowly. How would I explain this one? It placed the term "young, hot mom" on a totally new level. We could be sisters instead. That'd be more believable. But how is it that she hadn't aged while waiting in this time-capsule sort of garden? Had my body aged in Mr. Rose's closet for a few weeks?

"You really don't remember anything?" I asked.

She waited as if weighing her words. "You said your name is Pero?"

I nodded. "Dad picked out my name because he likes Old English names, and you liked the meaning behind it. It's the root word for *feather*."

I grasped for the feather pendant around my neck but met

air instead. "I did have the pendant, but I left it in the sanctuary."

"What does it look like?"

"It's made of wood and has the word *koach* insribed on the back. It means strength."

Mom pulled out the same pendant from under her shirt. "You mean this one?"

I nodded. "The very same, except yours is in much better condition than mine."

"You're one of the chosen."

"Somehow, yes." I didn't want to bother explaining she'd adopted me. That'd confuse the situation even more. If we had to stay in here for a long time, there was plenty of time. But if we never aged and came back through the curtain thirty years from now, I'd still be my seventeen-year-old self and Henry would be...a definite, forever *no*.

"You really are my daughter," she said.

"Uh, sure."

"Well, you'd have to be. The prophecy says it'll be three chosen of Abram blood." Mom paced. "How else would you have found this garden if Elohim didn't give you the power? Especially without the necklace." Mom paced more. "You said *Dad*, like I had a...a husband." She stopped. "I think I remember having a husband. Sol. No. It was some fish's name."

"Salmon?"

Mom looked hopeful. "Yes! He's your father?"

I rubbed my head. Why did my family have to be so complicated? "It's a long story, and I promise to tell you. But first I want to hear how you got through to the other universe." I didn't see any closets in the garden. There were no trees with doors.

"What other universe?" She didn't remember anything.

"What's the machine thingy you were talking about?"

"I thought the machine would take me somewhere else."

"It did, otherwise I wouldn't be here. You lived a whole life in Origo. So where is the machine?"

Mom led me near the edge of the garden where the brush thickened. She moved branches and leaves out of the way and revealed a white, circular machine that reminded me of a concrete mixer. Would the only way to get out of here be to travel back to the older universe?

"It's not working," Mom said. "I've tried to get through the last couple of weeks, but nothing. I don't understand. It's the only entrance to anything in this place." She looked around as if something would appear to give her another way out.

"Elohim wanted me here. I heard you singing."

Mom's face scrunched. "I wasn't singing."

"The lullaby. You know." I sang the refrain.

"That's an old song passed down from Abram for the Lesaries."

"But you didn't sing it in the last couple days?"

Mom shook her head. "You wouldn't want me to. I have a terrible singing voice."

I sighed. "I remember."

A distant cry alerted my senses. I scanned around me. "Do you hear that?"

"Yes, I do. Sounds like a baby." Mom jumped back and dropped her necklace to the ground. "The pendant is hot."

The baby's cry disappeared, and in its place, the machine whirred to life.

"It's working!" Mom hustled to the machine. "I'll go first, you follow."

"You sure about this?"

"Of course, I am."

"Okay." I waved. "See you on the other side."

I pushed myself through the cement mixer looking thing after Mom, the fiery pain feeling longer than a few seconds. I crashed on dust and twigs. Lifting myself up, I brushed the dirt from my hands. Remnants clung to the left-over slime from the water I'd dropped into. I really needed a bath.

A forest surrounded me and a vast field spread to the edge of the trees. Light fog, dew on the grass, and grey skies revealed a new day. In the middle of the field stood a small, wood cabin. Smoke poured out from its chimney, and a single light shone through its window.

Mom—a few feet away from me—took off in a run.

It didn't take long to catch up. "Where are you going?"

A bright smile lit her face. "I remember where I am. I'm going home."

I stopped running. She didn't belong here. It wasn't the apartment where Mom had first met Dad, wasn't Moon City, and it certainly wasn't our house in Green Meadow. Where else was left?

Salmon.

But Mom's first husband—Sam's dad—had died long ago. Who lived there now?

"Mom," I whispered loudly. "I mean, Bahar." I raced until I caught up to her, pulling her arm to stop her.

Her eyes lit up like fire.

"It's not who you think. Salmon—he doesn't live there anymore."

Mom glared, which coming from someone who couldn't be any older than nineteen didn't have as much threat as it did when it came from older-looking Mom.

"My husband lives here."

I shook my head. "He—he died. There was an accident a long time ago, and he didn't make it."

"How am I supposed to believe you? You come out of nowhere, claim to be my daughter, then I finally remember where I am, and you tell me it's not real."

I wanted to cry. It'd be so much easier if Mom could start

again, if Salmon hadn't died and she lived happily with her husband and their son. I would've been left under that tree, and the prophecy would've been passed on to some other lucky person. I didn't deserve to be chosen.

"I'm sorry." Tears threatened to spill.

Mom's face softened. She squeezed my hand and scanned me as if I were a puzzle she didn't have the pieces to. "Have faith, Pero."

Mom yanked me toward the house in a half-walk, half-gallop. When we were close enough for me to smell freshly baked bread, I broke free. "We should at least take a peek to make sure it's Salmon."

Mom dipped her head. "If it makes you feel better."

We shuffled below the window, and Mom peered above the sill.

"See anyone?" I whispered.

Mom pulled away. "No. But he may be in the barn. I think I'll take a look inside the cabin first, though."

"Are you sure? What if it's not him?"

"I'll be okay."

She approached the front door before I could stop her. When she turned around and motioned for me to come, I shook my head. She shrugged her shoulders and walked in, closing the door behind her.

A crash came from behind the house. I wanted to warn Mom, but she might be safer in the empty house. I snuck around to the back of the house and heard more noise coming from the barn.

Running through the grass, I stopped when I'd reached the edge of the barn and crouched at the entrance.

"Can't he send someone else?" A woman's voice sounded mature, around Mom's age. Well, like my version of Mom anyway.

The gentle purr of an animal answered, then a younger

man's voice. I knew that voice, but I had to be imagining things. There's no way *he* would be here. "Ima, it's going to be okay. An angel of Elohim appeared to Shea. This isn't anyone asking for my help. It's Elohim Himself."

I heard a heavy sigh from the woman, whose voice also sounded familiar. "It's too risky. Moon City doesn't have a good reputation for keeping people alive."

Moon City? Had I heard correctly? Maybe Carper had built another Moon City when I wasn't looking.

"If Elohim is with me, then I don't have to fear," the man's voice said. "I'm leaving in an hour, before it's too hot. I'll be at the camp with the Lesaries when I'm done with this mission, and if you come with me, then you'll be there too. I don't want you to stay here alone."

"I'm not afraid," she said. "It won't happen again."

"You don't know that. Someone could easily find us. But that's not what I'm concerned about. I don't think it's good for you to be alone. Elohim would want us to be with His people. When was the last time you talked with other women?"

No one responded.

"You need to come," he said. "So that you can be with the Lesaries when I return and not worry so much. Elohim wants us to spy on the land, get an idea of what we're up against before we march around the walls, then leave. Henry will be with me."

I shifted at the mention of Henry's name. My foot made a rustling sound against a leaf. Did they hear me?

"So grown up" the woman's voice said. "Your—"

"Shh," the man's voice said. "Someone's here."

I looked around. I could run back to the house, but Mom and I would both be stuck inside. Maybe I could find my way to China again.

"Must be an animal," the woman said.

"I don't think so," the man said.

Whoever was in this barn had really good perception skills. I took a big breath. Too late to hide. "Don't hurt me. I'm stepping out."

I tip-toed into the barn and took in the surprised faces of Sam and Alexis and the large eagle, Faith.

19

停顿

Faith made a loud "*caw*" and craned her neck while backing up.

Sam rubbed the giant feathers on her neck, which rose above Sam's head.

"Faith, it's me. Pero."

Her black, round eyes appeared wise next to the curve of her golden beak.

I closed my jaw, which had somehow opened wide. "What are you two doing here?"

Sam and Alexis looked at each other, then back at me.

"Do we know you?" Sam asked.

Great. How did I know everyone so far on this small farm, yet nobody could remember me? It was like *Back to the Future*, only in another universe.

"I'm Pero Moshe." I tried to pull on the necklace as if to ask for entrance into a secret club. Necklace wasn't there. Access denied. Where was a celebrity friend to vouch for me when I needed one? Like Carper. Or David Copperfield. "I did have the necklace. It's complicated. But so you believe me, it's made of wood and has *koach* inscribed on the back."

Alexis and Sam glanced at each other.

"I'm sort of a descendant of Abram." I grimaced. "Another complicated story."

I could tell by the shock on their faces that they still didn't recognize me. If they couldn't get past this news, how would I tell them that Bahar was probably eating bread in their kitchen and was in fact Sam's biological mom? If I *had* landed in the past and Sam was about to travel to Moon City with Henry to find Bahar, the time was about three months prior. That would've been before I'd found Mom and met Henry.

"I'll explain eventually," I said. "But I do need to tell you that there's a group of Lesaries in China who really need a place to come where they can hide. If they don't, they'll be turned in and end up in prison or dead, and I can't live with that guilt. They've been trapped for so long, and Elohim sent me to rescue them. I don't know why I ended up here. I was just trying to find my mom, and I did, but she was the younger version of herself because she went back to her old hiding place in the Forbidden City when going through the tree in this world." They stared at me blankly. Couldn't I keep my mouth shut? "Back to the Lesaries in China. I was thinking, if we could get them through a garden where I found my mom and through..."

They zoned out at something behind me before I could explain the machine, not that they understood a word I said. I turned around to see what had their attention. Mom ran through the grass from the house at full speed.

"Salmon!" she hollered.

She'd lost it. I would've, too, if my body had been stuck in a garden for thirty years.

As she approached the entrance to the barn, Mom stopped and stared at Sam, her face turning white. "You're not Salmon."

Poor Mom. She had to feel lost, landing in a place she

thought was home, only to have it be another wall to close her in.

"I'm sorry. From a distance, you looked just like him."

Sam wrinkled his brow. "Salmon died when I was young. I'm his son. And you are...?"

Mom blinked in surprise. "That can't—" She released a small sound, then closed her mouth and rubbed her head. Her eyes brightened as she laughed.

I placed a hand on her arm. "Mom, are you alright?"

"Did you just call her *mom*?" Alexis asked.

"I'm not your mom!" Mom ran for the woods, her voice trailing behind her. "I want to go home."

"Wait!" Sam ran after her.

Alexis and I followed.

"It's not safe in those woods," Sam said. "You can get lost."

I hadn't gotten lost in the woods. Well, unless you count coming out of a tree and into the forest. Okay, I was lost.

Mom pressed on.

I ran, passed Alexis and Sam, and caught up to Mom at the edge of the forest. "We can talk this through." I stopped and rested my hands on my knees. "It's a lot to understand. I know."

"You don't understand." Tears streamed down her face.

I'd never seen Mom break down. It wasn't very pretty, even on a young, pretty lady. Had she broken down like this with Carper? I imagined her feelings would've been suppressed for a long time under his control. Yet Carper's dinner party in Moon City had shown a spunky side of Mom I hadn't expected. There was still so much I didn't know about her.

Alexis came close and brought her arm around Mom. "Let's find a place to sit in the house and talk. A loaf just came out of the oven."

"Alexis makes the best bread."

Alexis studied me. "Let's go inside and figure all this out."

How would talking help anyone when nothing I'd say would make sense?

"Stop!" Mom shouted. "Don't you see? This is not your home. It's *mine*. Salmon built this house, and I found him here first. He's supposed to be here. But then there's this young man —" She pointed to Sam. "—who looks nearly identical to Salmon, but there's something different about him, and I'm supposed to believe that he's Salmon's son. And this lady over here is supposed to be my daughter. And you—" She pointed to Alexis. "I don't know who you are. But it doesn't matter. I escaped the garden, away from Carper, and this is where I am. I'm home. So, if you all would leave me here where I belong, I would greatly appreciate it."

She breathed heavily. Her shoulders bobbed up and down and her arms shook. The Mom I'd met in Carper's mansion always looked to Elohim, no matter the circumstances. That mom was calm, even in the storm. But this woman—with flowy and lush black hair and a naturally tan complexion— was a young woman who'd recently been abused by none other than Dr. Calvin Carper. This fear revealed a woman who'd missed seeing Moon City's walls tumble because she was swept away through a portal just before Elohim performed the miracle. The anxiety uncovered a woman who thought it easier to re-live the beautiful past, to hold on and not let go if it meant you never had to face the difficult again. Even if that memory was lonely. Even if it wasn't real. Salmon was the most real thing she'd ever known. More than Dad and me. More than the garden where she'd hid. More than the walls of Moon City where she'd been held hostage. More than her nickname, Rahab. This was who she identified herself as, before she claimed her name Bahar as its rightful definition: *spring*.

Because she didn't want to spring forward into something new. She wanted to stay in the happiest part of her life: loved and cherished by a man named Salmon who was the closest to Elohim she'd ever find.

How had Mom transformed from fear in her youth to faith when I met her years later? Had Elohim worked so deeply in her?

I glanced at Sam and paused when I noticed his eyes focused on me.

The same spark I'd felt when I first saw him ignited.

He didn't remember me or that at one point very soon he'd see me again trapped in Moon City. Days later, he'd learn we were both part of the chosen three. He'd think we were siblings, and a few days later, he'd learn we weren't related. He'd wonder why Elohim would choose me when I clearly didn't genetically belong.

But right then, Sam saw me for the first time, like the first first-time: a girl with a gift that united us in a deeper way than I'd ever felt with Henry. A gift that once used, would change this universe and the next. A gift that I prayed would bring us back to the sanctuary so that Elohim's people could be free once more.

When Sam's gaze remained on mine, I recognized that our connection was more than an initial spark at the first or second or whatever number of meetings this was. Because no matter where I ended up, I always seemed to land near this man. And that was enough to make me wonder if Sam himself was my destiny.

Then I heard a baby cry.

I lifted my head and strained my ear. "Where is that cry coming from?"

Alexis stepped forward. "She's in the house. I'll get her in a minute."

In the house? But I heard a baby cry from the woods, and it was the same cry Mom and I had heard from the garden. This had to mean something.

"Where is she?" I asked.

"I can get Ruth," Alexis said. "She's a baby." She said it as if I'd never heard of tiny human beings before.

She hurried toward the house as I stepped into the woods.

"Don't go in there." Sam pulled on my arm.

"It's not safe," I said. "I heard you before. But I think the cry is coming from the forest, and I really need to find out what it means."

"Right here," Mom said.

I looked over to where Mom had walked a few feet into the woods. Underneath the tree was a baby. Mom leaned down to pick her up, and she stopped crying.

"How did Ruth end up there?" Sam moved closer to Mom, scanning the trees as if they were as alive as the statue soldiers. "We need to get out of here."

Déjà vu rushed through my mind: Mom, Sam, Alexis, tree, baby.

Me.

What was happening? It couldn't be the past. That couldn't be me. I was standing right here. The cry, the lullaby, us coming here, Sam. There had to be a connection. But pasts didn't collide with futures, or the present. What time was it, anyway?

A flash of light directed my attention to a gaping hole that had opened in the tree.

"Nooo!" Alexis screamed from across the field. I heard the rush of her feet against the tall grass, felt the slam of Sam nearly knocking me over as he charged forward. My knees gave way, and I knelt on the ground and watched in horror as the tree swallowed Mom and the baby, closing behind.

Gone.

Alexis clung to the tree and sobbed. Sam hung his head, gathered Alexis into his arms, and squeezed her tight. I clung to the ground as if it would hold me. Like Mom did when she took that baby—me—into our future.

Why did Sam and Alexis keep me here as a baby?

One thing was clear. I needed to learn where I'd come from, not only to find a safe place to return the Lesaries in China, but to find myself, to learn that the baby part of me wasn't just a ghost from the past who floated in-between arms. I had a story. And I was determined to find out how I'd begun.

20

放心

Alexis stomped toward me in a fury. I stepped back. Sam got hold of Alexis' shirt and locked her in his strong arms.

"What'd you do with Ruth?" Alexis screamed at my face. Spit flew like sparks from her mouth.

"It's not my fault!" I lifted my hands in frustration. "I know I sound crazy, but—"

"You and that lady appeared out of thin air and took..." She choked on a sob, crumbled to the ground, and tucked her head low like a snail in its shell.

Pain settled in Sam's eyes.

"Sam." Tears surfaced. "I'm sorry." I took off into the woods.

Sam called out and ran after me.

Sam wasn't as fast as Henry, so he wouldn't be able to keep up, but if he caught me, his arms would be strong enough to keep me there. Maybe that's what I wanted. Instead, I pressed on.

Why, Elohim? Was my heart not broken enough? Did it have to be shattered in more pieces? I broke their hearts, too.

I kicked a tree. When my foot responded in pain, I lowered

myself against the trunk and breathed heavily, letting the burn from the run have its full effect.

Too many doors and closets came from trees. Sam carved wood from them and made special things, like guitars that brought magic and whatever other trinkets carpenters made in their spare time. Ducks, perhaps. Each item Sam made had a purpose. His carvings became door after dang door that led places. But I was tired of going places and spinning in circles without a door that blinked *Exit* in neon green.

I heard the shuffling of feet on leaves before I saw Sam approach. Knowing his ability to be ninja-like, I guessed he'd been loud intentionally so he wouldn't startle me. Thoughtful Sam leaned against a tree and folded his arms. Without the plaid shirt that I would choose for him when shopping with Henry, his billowing white pants and tan shirt gave him a foreign look. Handsome still, yes, but not resembling Eddie Bauer in any way.

"You think I'm crazy." I stared at the tree tops; some wore green hats, others red and orange. Sam and I had chatted under a sky in the forest not too long ago. He seemed to know my thoughts, to perceive the parts of me that I didn't even know existed. I lifted my head and met his gaze. There were those big brown eyes, the same as before. But without him aware of our short history—what he'd known about me and what I'd known about him—all I sensed was curiosity.

"I believe you." Sam's words felt complete, like he'd swallowed them and was satisfied.

I leaned my head against the trunk. "No, you don't, Sam Nesim." My voice was soft and quiet.

When he didn't reply, I looked back at him. Why did he study me so intently? As if I was the first girl he'd ever seen.

"There's something about you. It's a power in you. Strength."

I didn't avert my eyes and remembered why I'd liked him in

the first place. Sam: the man who knew me and everything I'd become with just one look.

"Koach."

Sam smiled. "You really are a chosen." He believed me without needing to ask.

"So are you."

Sam nodded his head slightly with a light chuckle. "You *have* met me." He crouched down so that his forearms rested on his legs. "What I don't get is how you know me so well, yet I've never met you in my life. I would've remembered you."

I smiled at his compliment. "I'm sure you still do, back in the younger universe."

Sam sighed, then stood. "I used to live on Earth when I was a teen. I stayed with my uncle in a small town."

"It's at the Oregon coast, near Green Meadow where I grew up." I nodded. "Green Meadow is also where I left you. You were about to plant a garden there."

The sound of Sam's laugh fell on my ears like a refreshing drizzle.

"That's something I'd do."

"Your uncle, Mr. Rose, is after the chosen."

"He has been for a while. Uncle Rose is more of a distant relative to me, but his wicked heart is the reason I left Earth and returned here." Sam paced, then sat crisscross and face-to-face with me. He set his elbows on his knees and inter-laced his fingers as a place to rest his chin. "Pero, it sounds like we knew each other well in your world. Were we..."

My face flushed. "Not exactly."

"Hmm." Sam looked away and nodded his head. "I'm supposed to leave for Moon City. The leader of the Lesaries asked for me and another guy to spy on the land."

"I know that, too."

His eyes brightened.

"That's why my mom disappeared. She had to live the rest

of her life so that she could wait inside the Moon City wall in time. You and Henry will meet her there. You'll tie a red scarf that Bahar will tear in half and tie to her window so that you know where she is later. But when you return for her, you'll find me instead. And that's where we'll meet. We won't have any recollection of this moment, that we met or anything. At least, I won't. I guess I don't know about you." What if Sam had remembered me when I first met him? He could've not said anything. Hadn't he said I seemed familiar to him? "Who's Ruth?"

Sam exhaled into his palms. Whatever it was he needed to say, I sensed its heavy weight. "I can't share anything about where she came from."

But he had to tell me. If Ruth *was* me, I needed to know. My middle name was Ruth, after all. Who were my birth parents? Had I appeared in their lives like I had appeared for Mom and Dad? I resisted the urge to press.

"Why do you want to know about Ruth?"

I couldn't say it. He'd believed me so far, but this was too out there. I wasn't sure if I could believe it myself.

"You can talk to me, Pero."

I cleared my throat and sat up straighter. "I think... Don't freak out, but I think that Ruth is me. *Ruth* is my middle name, and I was found under a tree as a baby."

Sam shook his head. "But baby Ruth isn't one of the chosen. Her birth mother isn't..." He leaned back and set his hands on the dirt, letting his eyes study a red mushroom nearby. "I've said too much."

"I'm not related to the Abram family."

Sam's head shifted back to me so quickly that I had to hold back a laugh. His face looked relieved. Perhaps he once again thought that if we were both chosen that we must be related.

I felt like I was in one of those romcom movies where the guy said, if we could start over, what would you think of me and the girl responded with, I'd love you. When Henry had asked me a similar question, I'd responded that I thought we might kill each other either way. I didn't mean it literally. I'd never hate Henry enough to be cruel. Yet sitting in front of Sam—him possibly thinking he might stand a chance with me like he did in the past, him not knowing anything about me and Henry—maybe this was my second chance. Not in a romantic kind of way. But to sit across from each other as we did then and enjoy the moment without drama.

Like I did with Yeshua by the river. If Mom hadn't taken me as a baby, I would've grown up in the little cabin next to the magical woods, then with Shea and the Lesaries. Would Mom have been rescued from Moon City if I'd never gone to another world? Would I have found younger Mom in the Forbidden City?

No.

I was chosen for a reason. Whether I figured out why I had been here as a baby and where I'd come from was up to Elohim. Right now, my purpose for visiting the past was to get Sam's permission to bring the Lesaries to safety. "I need your help."

We approached the tree I'd come through. The opening was still there, a mystic fog swirling into the void.

Sam placed both hands on the tree and bowed his head in prayer. He lifted his head and let go. "There. That should keep access open for when you bring the Lesaries back through. I felt Elohim's power move through me."

"Thank you." I touched the tree but didn't feel anything. "Now I need to figure out how to bring them here."

"I'll pray for your safety."

I smiled, then moved a twig with my foot. "Will Alexis be okay?"

Sam's face grew dim. "It will be difficult, but we'll make it."

"Trust me. As someone who knows what will happen, it will work out."

Sam nodded.

"I am curious." I moved the twig back and forth with my foot, then paused. "If I really am Ruth, how is it that I meet you years later when I'm older and you're the same age? If you are still twenty-three."

He smiled. "I'll be twenty-three next month. How old are you?"

I hesitated. If only I could make that gap a little smaller. "Seventeen."

Was that a grimace? "Younger than I thought. Time is different in the two universes. Origo is slower than Earth, so it's very likely that during the time you grew up on Earth, I stayed roughly the same age. Or maybe Elohim froze time in one place. I guess it's possible."

"I don't know why He'd do that." Why stop time so that I could catch up to Sam in age? Would that happen again if I stayed in Origo while Sam was in Green Meadow?

"I don't always understand His ways either, but I have a theory."

"What's that?"

"You know." He scratched his chin. "From the other part of the prophecy."

"The Lesarie leader, Jehoshua, brought that up, too."

"Do you think it's for..." Sam pointed to me, then him. "...us?"

"For *us* how?"

"The part about three generations being the chosen. It started with my mom, then me, and will be my future son or daughter."

It wasn't me? All this time, I wasn't one of the three chosen? "But I was given a power through music. I see visions. One vision helped me fly, for goodness' sake."

Sam looked panicked. "You didn't know, did you?"

I shook my head.

Sam rubbed his temple. "And now I've told you something you weren't ready to hear."

"Jehoshua's words exactly."

He groaned. "I'm sorry, Pero. I thought you'd know the rest of the prophecy."

"Now I do, but I don't get it. Why did my mom give me the necklace if she knew I wasn't one of the chosen?"

"She must've seen the calling in you. She knew you were the one to carry on the lineage to the promised Messiah."

Yeshua's words to me next to the river rushed into my mind. *One of your future children will be the descendant leading up to my coming.*

It was confusing at the time. I was only seventeen and was far from thinking about having children.

"I thought the three chosen would bring the Messiah."

"They will."

"Then how can—oh." All this time—Mom finding me as a baby and bringing me in, the prophecies, visions, necklaces, sync between the chosen three—my gift directly pointed to unity with the chosen. Not by blood. "Through marriage."

Sam's face turned pink. "The same thing happened to my father, Salmon. He began to see visions. Elohim spoke to him and used him in craftsmanship to build shelter for my mom who was one of the chosen three."

"It all connects, like pieces being joined together without limitations of time or age or skill. Elohim makes it happen...if we say 'yes'."

Sam nodded. "No one's asking you to agree to anything right now."

Right now. Sam was giving me space, but still there was an invitation to join what he might have known all along.

"Is that why you proposed to me?"

Sam looked up. "I did?"

"Right after you found out that I wasn't your sister because we didn't share the same mom."

Sam grimaced. "That was hasty of me. I should've explained more before doing something like that. Maybe I'll remember this second time around." He smiled. "The point is, I'm not asking you to marry me. Elohim could still fulfill what He promised no matter what happens between us."

Did he not want me? Or was he trying not to pressure me into anything I didn't want? But I didn't know what I wanted, which was why I'd paused with Henry.

"I'm unsure what the future holds, Sam. But right now, Elohim wants me to wait. I'm still in high school, and a lot has changed. I want time with my dad and mom, if she ever returns to us."

Sam nodded. "You're speaking with wisdom." He slapped the tree. "It sounds like I'll see you again soon, Ruth." He winked.

A grin spread wide. "Looking forward to it. Bye, Sam." I hesitated, wondering if it would be appropriate to give him a hug. I reached out my hand instead. Why'd I do that? As if we were business partners or something.

He took my hand, but instead of a shake, he held it. His grip was firm yet gentle. A surge rushed through me, like an electric shock. I understood why we shared a connection at every touch, every look. Sam was my soul mate in order to be a significant part of Elohim's purpose.

When the time came for me to decide to commit to a marriage basically arranged by God Himself, would I say 'yes'?

Sam let go.

I stepped into Mom's shadow, leaving my future behind.

21

———

上升

I landed on my feet with a thud. In the garden, the brick wall leading to the shrine was open. I peeked beyond the curtain. A guard tied Henry's hands behind his back. Time had to be different between the two worlds, otherwise Henry would've been gone a while ago.

Mr. Rose entered the room and slapped Henry's cheek with a smack that echoed off the walls.

Henry groaned and bent his head to the side. Wet curls mangled against his forehead.

I resisted rushing over to tuck them behind his ears, find an ice pack for his cheek, and tell him it'd be okay. But nothing was okay. I'd returned to rescue him and the Lesaries and now had to confront Rose. I couldn't leave him there.

Rose smacked Henry across the other cheek.

I grimaced, then ran through the open wall and into the room. "You will let him go!"

Rose smiled. "Lucky for your boyfriend, you were just who we were looking for."

Maybe I hadn't made the best choice by entering.

Rose paraded around me in a full circle before standing right before me. "Now. Only two more to go. Where's Calvin?"

"Where do you think?" I asked. "With the Lesaries."

It wasn't a secret. The guards knew where the sanctuary was hidden and that the only way to get them out was to find Mom, but now that Mom was gone for maybe another 14 years, we all were in trouble. Either that or time would do a fancy warp thingy and freeze us until Mom returned.

So not likely.

"How do we reach Calvin?" Rose asked.

"The only way is with my mom, and she is missing." Telling the truth wouldn't get him anywhere. We were both at a dead end.

"How do I know she's not behind that wall you appeared from?" He raised a brow as if he'd voiced the smartest words he'd ever said.

"Already checked. She's not there."

"Show me."

"The wall closed behind me."

"You heard me." He popped his knuckles. "Take me through the wall."

That wasn't such a good idea, if the machine worked. The last thing I wanted was for him to find a way into the other world. Escaping there with the Lesaries was their greatest chance of survival.

"Why do you want to find her so badly?"

Rose grunted. "Teens think they need to know everything."

"Even if I wanted to, I can't get you through the wall, Mr. Rose."

He glared. "Try."

I gulped and glanced at Henry. One eye was already swelled shut, and his cheek had turned purple. He managed a slight smile, but the swelling made it impossible to see his dimple.

Elohim, help him.

I placed my hand against the wall. It warmed like it had before. "Put your hand on my shoulder."

Rose shrank back. "No games?"

"If you want to find my mom, you're going to have to take a chance with me."

He lifted his hand, hesitated, then set it on my shoulder. Pain intensified and a door opened.

He looked at me and back to the door, laughing with excitement. "This is incredible."

The guard talked rapidly in Chinese.

"Gentlemen first," I said.

Ignoring me, Rose stepped through. I rolled my eyes and followed. The guard pulled Henry along behind me.

"This is magical." Rose turned slowly with eyes aglow. "Take a look at those fruit trees!" He picked up an apple from a tree and bit into it.

Dumb man. What if it was poisonous?

"Delicious." He wiped his mouth with the back of his hand.

"What's that?" Rose pointed to the white machine.

Great. Another language to translate. "I'm not sure. Seems to be some kind of concrete spinny thingy."

Rose examined the machine.

The guard spoke more Chinese.

"It's a time machine," the one-eyed, purple-cheeked Henry said.

Both Rose and I looked up at once.

"Is that so?" Rose asked.

I shook my head at Henry. *No*, I mouthed.

"It'll take you to another universe."

Apparently, Henry still hadn't learned to read my lips. He'd figured out how to kiss them, but that was beside the point. Why was he telling Rose this? And how did he know? He wasn't here when the machine squashed me and my same-aged mother.

Henry translated to the guard. The guard perked up and forgot about Henry completely, approaching the machine with Rose to inspect.

When Henry slowly started to back up, I got it. His plan wouldn't work. They'd catch up to us.

"We're fast runners," Henry whispered.

I whispered back. "I'm fastest...faster. Whatever."

"How does it work?" Rose asked.

"A button on the side," I said.

"I see it!"

"Press it."

"You do it." Rose looked up, and Henry froze. Rose turned to the guard. "Bring him closer. Don't want anyone taking off."

The guard didn't move.

"Want me to translate?" Henry moved closer to Rose.

"I'll press the button." I walked over to the machine, found the switch, and flipped it. My hand started to warm from the machine, and the machine started to hum.

"It's working!" Rose said.

Oh, no. It wasn't supposed to work without Mom here.

"This has to be the entrance to find Bahar and that other guy." Rose talked with the guard who nodded his head rapidly. "Once we have the three chosen and Carper, we'll bring them to the lab."

Is that what this was all about? Rose wanted to use us as experiments in Carper's old lab, possibly to dictate the world as Carper had tried before Moon City fell to pieces. But our powers wouldn't work if Elohim didn't allow them to, right? I didn't want to find out.

I backed up until I bumped into Henry. He grabbed my hand and took off with me to the wall. The guard saw us first and ran after us, using who-knew what kind of angry words. The guard gained speed but not enough.

I slammed into the wall, pressing my hand against it. The

brick wall opened into the shrine room. Grabbing Henry by the shirt, I jerked us into the room. The walls slowly started to close.

"Can't it go any faster?" I asked.

The guard reached the opening and stuck his foot through the wall. The rest of his body squeezed through, and the door shut behind him. He tripped over the curtain and fell to the floor.

Rose slammed against an invisible barrier, then yelled a profanity in Chinese.

"Excuse your French." I stuck out my tongue, and the wall closed to solid brick.

We left from behind the curtain. The swirling gold fog made it impossible to see the guard.

"Let's get out of here."

I kept up a steady pace with Henry through the halls of the Forbidden City. The guard was nowhere in sight. The fog had lifted. No sign of walking statues.

"How'd Mr. Rose find us, anyway?"

"Pure luck." Henry paused. "Why'd you come back so soon? You were only gone for a couple seconds."

"Stop talking. I'm trying to run."

"Not the old I'm-not-talking-to-you phase." Henry panted. "We know each other too well for that."

Maybe I didn't want to talk with him. I thought I'd been teasing, but was I?

"What happened in there, Ro girl?"

I wished he'd stop calling me that. I'd started to like it when he made up the nickname, but I couldn't shake off my growing irritation. What was getting to me?

Sam.

Seeing him again made me feel off. Like all I wanted to do in the Forbidden City was find the sanctuary, get the Lesaries to safety, and see what happened to Sam and Ruth. Why had I landed at his little cabin by the woods right when the baby was taken away? Why had the other part of the prophecy made me feel like I'd flown to a wishing star and the wish had come true?

"You can stop, Pero," Henry said. "No one's chasing."

I halted when I realized he'd stayed behind me.

"What's wrong?"

I focused on my breath until it was steady. "I saw a cabin in the woods. Mom was there, but she was young and didn't remember. No one remembered me."

"Who else was there?"

"Alexis and a baby named Ruth." I pursed my lips, refusing to mention the other person. I couldn't do that to Henry.

"Who else?"

Gosh, he knew me too well! I rubbed the back of my neck. "Uh...Sam."

"I see." Henry withdrew. "But they didn't remember you."

"Correct."

"So, Sam didn't remember that he thought you two might be related."

"Something like that." I sighed. "Henry, can we stop talking about this?"

He pressed on. "And you're confused because you think you might still be in love with him."

The heat on my cheeks had to be close to Henry's purple bruise. "I didn't say that."

Henry's face fell as if I had. He walked forward at a quick pace. "Let's keep going. I have an idea of what could get us into the sanctuary."

"Henry."

He picked up his pace. "It would've been easier if your mom had come with us. But we'll figure it out."

I stomped my foot on the ground and folded my arms. "Henry Beggs, stop walking!"

He slumped, making him appear even more bruised. I lifted his shoulders and looked into his eyes.

"Don't ever think I don't value you. And Sam too. You two have been friends for a lot longer than we have. But as your friend, I will always, always want you by my side."

Henry shook his head. "You say that, Ro, but it's not the same."

I gently touched the tender part of his cheek. He grimaced, and I backed away. "Why can't we go back to the way we used to be?"

"You mean when you ignored me and called me your annoying bodyguard?"

I smiled. "I liked you. I just didn't know how to show it."

Henry frowned. "You sure do change your mind a lot."

I didn't want to agree, but he was right. I'd been on an emotional carousel since I'd heard that Mom was alive and I was to find her. It wasn't fair to Henry, nor Sam.

Ugh! Seventeen was too hard! If only I were twenty. Then I'd have far more answers than questions. I was sure of it.

A woman's shout from around the corner jolted me awake. I did a double take as she came into view, her arms at her sides, her stride faster than I thought possible for a forty-something year old.

"Mom?"

"Pero! Henry!" Older Mom caught up to us and zoomed past. "Run!"

When the guard and Rose stumbled around the corner, Henry and I took off at full speed.

22

———————

收集

"**W**elcome back," I said to Mom. Since when had she become a fast runner?

A bullet shot through the air, a couple of inches near my head. Mom and I screamed.

"Turn right!" Henry shouted.

We swerved to the right as another gunshot echoed through the hall, and the guard yelled in Chinese.

My whole body pounded with adrenaline.

Henry opened a door in the hall, and we scurried inside, Henry closing the door behind him. Shouts carried from the hall we'd just escaped from. I started when I heard commotion behind me and turned to a mob of tourists watching us from behind a rope. A sign nearby read, "*Do not walk on king.*"

What king? I took in our surroundings. A gold chair sat at the end of a red carpet.

Holy cadoodles, our shoes were eroding a historical landmark. Dad would be furious.

A guard yelled at us from behind the rope. Even he wouldn't dare walk on the king. We scurried from the emperor's room and climbed over the rope, Henry saying what I assumed was *sorry*.

Mom and I sped forward.

"Slow down," Henry murmured.

We wouldn't want to draw more attention from the tourists, especially after Henry's grand performance as a magician earlier.

The same guard who'd caught us walking on the king kept stride with Henry.

"You, David Copperfield."

Wonderful. We were famous, and not in a good way.

"*Bu*." Henry said *no* in Mandarin.

The exit from the palace came in view. I wanted to run there, but the Chinese guard stayed in stride.

"You, David Copperfield."

A shout came from behind us.

"Stop them!"

Rose and the other guard pushed through the crowd far behind us. I turned back around to see that Mom had gained speed.

"Slow down," Henry said.

Mom and I took off in a run.

Henry had no choice but to follow. "We would've had a much better chance hiding."

We ignored him and focused all our energy on that run.

"I'll shoot," a guard shouted to our left.

He wouldn't dare shoot with all of these people around. But instead of being our shield, the people scattered so that we were an open target. A gun shot exploded through the air. People screamed and trampled over each other. My heart beat in triple time. Mom slowed down.

"Keep going."

She picked up speed again, wheezing.

The archway where Henry and I had grazed our hands

along the bumps for good luck was ahead. Henry touched one bump as he passed by.

In Tiananmen Square, under the intense gaze of Mao's portrait, Henry found a group of people and ducked himself into the middle. This time, Mom and I followed. Mom wheezed harder.

"You need water." There's no way she could keep running like this.

"Follow me," Henry said.

We crouched low and half-ran, half-walked to a section of the Tiananmen Tower. Deep inside the ground under our feet were the Lesaries, probably wondering where we'd gone. Henry looked over his shoulder, then crouched at a small window near the bottom of the tower. Henry tapped on the window, and it opened a couple seconds later.

"Henry!" a loud whisper came through the window. I could only see the top of someone's head but from the mass of black curls could tell it was Jehoshua. "The door's been opened! We can get through when you're ready."

Henry looked at Mom. "You opened it."

"What does that mean?" Mom asked.

I scanned around us. No sign of Rose and his yelling guard. "We don't have time. Let's get to the other side of the tower."

We found another group of tourists who held up their phones to take pictures of each person one at a time in front of the Mao portrait. When all looked clear, we traveled to the next group until we made our way through the gate, our heads down.

I led the way to the pagoda. When we arrived, its door opened wide. If someone passing by were to snoop around this area, they'd be able to see it clearly. We needed to get the people out of there before they were found.

Jehoshua pulled us in, giving Mom a quick hug that she couldn't return with her wheezing.

"She needs water."

Jehoshua said something in Chinese to a man near him, and the man returned a minute later with a wooden cup filled with water. Mom sat in a chair that was offered to her and took deep breaths. A woman approached Mom with a jar of oil and dabbed some on her forehead and her chest. Eucalyptus and peppermint filled the air. I took the biggest breath I had since being chased.

I turned to Jehoshua. "I know where we can go. It's a safe place, another world with land that can be ours. We can join the Lesaries there and be free."

"Where?" Jehoshua asked.

"Behind the wall in the shrine room. There's a garden and a machine that will take us there."

Jehoshua nodded. "We'll prepare right away."

I turned to check in with Henry, but he wasn't there.

"Where's Henry?" He'd been right by us the whole time. I sped for the door.

"I never saw him come in." Jehoshua put a hand on my arm. "Pero, it's not safe. We can't have anyone find us."

I felt panic settle on me, depriving me of oxygen. "I have to find him. Please. If I don't see him nearby, I'll come back. Give me an hour."

I didn't know if I could ever return without Henry. After all I'd been through with him, I needed him next to me.

"You should wait till morning. It will be dark soon," Jehoshua said.

Dad called my name. I rushed to him and gave a brief hug. "I need to find Henry. He's gone."

"I'll go with you."

I put my hand on his arm. "No, Dad. You need to stay with your wife."

Dad blinked. "My wife?"

I pointed at Mom who held her head and took deep

breaths. Mom pulled back her hair with her hands, lifting her head in the process, and froze when her eyes met Dad's. Her breathing became steady. Dad seemed to hold his own.

I'd imagined this scene my whole life, but it was far more magical than anticipated. The elation on Dad's face when he realized who was before him. The full smile on Mom's lips as Dad rushed by her side.

"Bahar." He touched a strand of her hair as if he thought holding too much might make her vanish. Then he touched her head, her cheek, and still, she did not leave. Mom closed her eyes for a moment, a single tear falling down her face.

I wiped a couple of tears and turned away, not wanting to intrude on such an intimate moment. They loved each other, after all these years. Their love had been real, and that was enough for me to know that someday very soon, we'd be happy once again.

I glanced around the room. Jehoshua had left. It was just me and my parents. They were so enamored with each other that they wouldn't notice me leave. I couldn't wait to find Henry. He could be hurt or taken.

I walked backward slowly until I met the wall, then slipped through the open door and into the warm night air.

23

———

哭

A block away from the Forbidden City; past the stand that sold fried scorpion; behind the artist at his canvas; in an alley surrounded by ancient looking brick buildings—I found him in a pool of blood.

"Henry!" I rushed to him.

He'd managed to pull off his shirt and tie it tightly to his head. He opened his eyes, then fluttered them closed again, his bare chest rising and falling.

"Henry, you need to stay awake."

"I *am* awake, Ro girl." He lifted a hand but let it drop as if it was too much work. "Don't yell for help. They'll find me."

Tears fell, and I wished he'd kiss them away. "How did this happen? You were right behind me."

"I was shot. Now, go."

"I'm not going to leave you, stubborn boy. Except to go get help."

"No." He coughed, and the hand he pulled away was splattered with blood.

"Henry, you're not going to make it if you don't get help." More tears came. This wasn't supposed to happen. He was fine.

He was right by me, the way it was supposed to be. Mom had been re-united with Dad; Cherry with Jehoshua. The Lesaries would run to freedom. Everyone was supposed to be happy. This was not happy.

"Go to the sanctuary, while...you...can." He closed his eyes again.

"Henry?" I felt for a heartbeat. His chest hair bathed my fingers in sweat.

"I'm alive."

"And you'll stay that way." I said it for my own comfort just as much as I did for him. "You're too stubborn to do anything other than that."

"You mean die?"

The word I'd avoided came easily from his mouth.

"I'm not afraid."

"Of course, you're not." I put my fingers against his forehead. It flamed with heat. "You're not afraid of anything. But that doesn't mean it should happen."

A sly smile lifted, revealing the dimple I wished would permanently stay.

"I'm calling for help, whether you like it or not."

Henry licked his lips. "Go ahead. I never could stop you."

"Help!" I stood and yelled out. "Somebody help me!"

No one came.

I'm here. Elohim's whispered promise came like a mist of ocean breeze. ***Blessed are those who mourn, for they shall be comforted.***

I didn't want to mourn. Why would Elohim say those words? This wasn't a blessing; it was a curse.

I took a deep breath in and with a shaky voice, sang Henry the lullaby that my mother—whoever she was—sang to me. But it wasn't a mother's song; it was Elohim's to His children.

"Even in your suffering, I am who I am."

Henry smiled, and I pretended that he wasn't fading, that Elohim would perform a miracle like I had witnessed many times before.

Henry lifted a shaky hand to my cheek and pulled my face forward until it was inches away from his. "Goodbye's not forever for us."

I cried into his hand, clutching it with mine.

"Ro girl," he whispered. "Thanks for letting your bodyguard be the first in line. You're not so hard to reach after all."

"I called 120 for an ambulance." Carper ran up from behind me. "They're on their way." Carper knelt down next to me.

I glanced at Carper, then back at Henry. "Don't you dare close your eyes. Help is here."

Henry continued to take one breath after another.

"How'd you know we were here?" I asked Carper.

"I saw you run into the alley and followed."

"What were you doing out of the sanctuary?"

"What were *you* doing away from the Lesaries? Do you realize how dangerous it is to walk on your own around here, let alone at night?"

"Not any more dangerous than being chased by Mr. Rose with a gun."

"Trust me, the man has no aim."

A siren sounded from a distance.

"They're here," I said.

"Finally." Henry sputtered. "You two..."

"No need to finish that sentence." I stood and ran to the front of the alley, waving my arms to direct the paramedics.

The white van—a red cross on the hood and the number 999 on the top—stopped. Four men in light blue scrubs emerged, rolling a stretcher down the ramp from back.

After talking with Carper in Mandarin, the paramedics moved Henry onto the stretcher and rolled him into the van.

I moved forward.

Carper held me back. "Let him go. I'll take you to see him tomorrow."

I yanked away from Carper's hold. "He might not even make it till tomorrow."

The paramedics closed the back doors, turned on their siren, and left.

I watched them drive out of sight and cried. I wiped tears with my shirt but stopped when I took in my shirt covered in dried dirt and Henry's blood. "I want my mom and dad."

Carper put his arm around my shoulder and led me in the direction of the Forbidden City. "Let's go find them."

I leaned on him for support, unable to carry on through my tears and weak muscles. Who cared if Carper couldn't be trusted. Right then, he was taking me to the ones I wanted to be with most. The ones who'd hold me and tell me it would be alright. But what if Carper wasn't really taking me back?

"Stop right there." Rose stepped out of the shadows and held a gun against my back.

You've got to be kidding. Didn't anyone take a vacation around here?

"Go ahead." I slumped my head. "I'm done running. And a gun isn't a threat when the shooter has bad aim."

Rose snatched me and held tight. "Stupid girl. If the gun is against your back, I don't need good aim.

"Let her go, Rose."

"I knew I needed to take care of this myself."

"Wait." I straightened and glared at Carper. "You were a part of this?"

"I changed my mind." Carper looked downcast.

"Too late for that." Rose tightened his grip on my wrist.

"You're the one who tried to kill Henry."

Carper didn't respond.

"Not man enough to admit it?"

"Shut up, Pero!"

"Why? Because you don't like people telling you the truth? Carper, you are a coward. You don't know how to love your daughter or how to stay loyal to friends. All because you want money."

Carper's chest heaved. "You're no better with your two boyfriends. When will *you* learn how to love?"

Fresh tears glistened. "Take it back."

"You know it's true."

"So what if it is? I *do* know how to love, but it hurts when everyone I love leaves me."

Carper scoffed. "Welcome to the club."

"Are we done yet?" Rose yanked my arm.

"You haven't shot the gun, so not really."

Rose lifted the firearm and fired into the air. "Listen to me!"

We stayed quiet. Passerby screamed and scattered. Guards surrounded, weapons ready.

I looked to the guards, then pointed to Rose. "This man is trying to take me!"

"Pero." Carper's tone was a warning.

"Arrest him!"

Rose snapped his finger. Two guards grabbed my arms from both sides. I squirmed, but their grip tightened.

Rose laughed under his breath. "Whose side did you think they'd be on? It's over, Pero. The world will soon be mine." Rose pointed to Carper and spoke in Chinese.

Carper's eyes widened, then he sped off.

Two guards chased after him, caught him, and brought him back.

"This wasn't part of the deal." Carper spit on the ground.

"You made a deal with Mr. Rose?"

"Yes, I did, and it was a mistake."

Rose grinned. "Seems like you would've learned not to trust me by now, Calvin. Although I must say, I kind of like a turn of being in charge."

Carper growled.

Rose dipped his head at the guards and pointed north. "To the palace." He muttered. "To a better future."

More like, to the end.

I hoped not.

24

———————

怀疑

We walked by the Tiananmen Tower. I squinted to glimpse any sign of the Lesaries through the small window. Someone's face peeked through. Was that Cherry? I stared as long as I could into the window. Maybe she'd see me and Carper. My parents were probably worried sick about me being gone. I should've listened to Jehoshua, but my prefrontal cortex must've been missing when I made the decision to run after Henry. Although, if I hadn't found Henry, he would'n't have made it.

Tiananmen Square was nearly empty, and one guard opened the gate to the palace now locked to tourists. No point in trying to break free when I was outnumbered.

The sun's rays cast orange and red, illuminating us like a spotlight as we passed the large clay pots and the house where the emperor's wives stayed; crossed a bridge over a small green lake with lily pads, dragonflies, and koi. Crossing several courtyards and pavilions, we entered a room with flower patterns painted on the floor and ceiling and mural of the city itself covering the entire wall.

A guard approached a square, raised platform with an elaborately colored rug. Perhaps it was used as a place to pray or meditate. The guard put both hands on the bottom of the platform and lifted, revealing a staircase that twisted down.

Carper groaned. "You found the lab."

"You made that easy," Rose said. "All it takes is one ring of the bell."

I bit my tongue to avoid a sarcastic response that I was sure would get me in more trouble. If I wasn't restrained, I would've run up to Carper and bit him too. Why did I trust him so easily?

"Can you let one of my hands loose for a second?"

The guards didn't turn their heads.

"I only want to smack myself. It won't take long."

Nothing. Not a blink.

I sighed, then followed Carper, Rose, and the guards underground.

My eyes blinked rapidly as I adjusted to the dim lighting. The platform at the top of the stairs shut behind us, reducing the lighting even further.

"I can hardly see." I'd die trying to get down the steep steps.

Rose said something in Chinese, and the guards let go.

"There's nowhere to run, Pero." Rose's eyes lasered on me. "Don't bother trying."

I glared. "I'm done running, remember?"

"When I'm finished experimenting, you'll be wishing you had tried."

I gulped. If I ran, they'd catch me in a millisecond. We were entering Carper's old lab where Mom had been tortured. My turn. Was I as strong as she?

Koach is within you.

Thank you, Elohim.

After traveling through enough halls to make me lost, the guards led me to a damp room, opened two empty cells side by side, and closed the doors. A dirt-smeared cot and basin were the only two luxuries.

"Welcome to your new home." Rose directed the guards to grab two blankets equally as dirty. They handed one to me and one to Carper.

"I need you alive tomorrow morning." He swiveled on his heel and walked out the door, the guards right behind.

I crinkled my nose. "A urine saturated blanket. How comforting."

Carper dropped it. "I wouldn't use it. Those things are covered with fleas."

I dropped the blanket as if it'd caught on fire and inspected the cot before sitting in the middle. It sagged and squeaked under pressure. So did I.

"This is all my fault." Carper sat on his cot so that we were back-to-back through the bars.

"You think?"

He sighed. "Look, I know you're mad at me, but if we're going to survive, you've got to listen."

"I did before, and look at us now. Moon City's rooms were better than this."

"That's my fault too. I designed this place."

I turned around and faced him. "Could've added a jacuzzi or some Van Gogh painting."

"Would you stop with the sarcasm?" Carper stood, then paced. "I messed up. I'm a failure. I don't know how to stay good."

"I'm no Shea or Shua, but I think the wise thing to say is that it's impossible to stay good."

"Thanks for the encouragement."

"No, I'm serious. It's not about if we're good enough; it's about Elohim."

Carper rubbed his head. "What if this whole thing is no use? Why would Elohim want me again?"

"I don't know, but for some reason He does."

"I don't even care about being king of anybody anymore. Money is one big game that no one wins. I quit."

"I quit too." No more running. No making decisions. "Just me, you, and Elohim stuck in a cell for the rest of our miserable lives."

"Hey." Carper faced me. "I didn't say we'd quit hoping. Don't ever do that, little girl. When you lose hope, you lose purpose. And when you lose purpose, you...I don't know. Something terrible happens. You rot, and nobody wants to be around you because you stink."

"I'm not a little girl, and I don't stink." I sniffed my arm, then coughed.

"I didn't mean it literally, Pero." He put both hands on the bars between us, leaned his head against them for a moment, and looked at me. "Ready to listen to my plan?"

"Hold on, I need to grab the popcorn."

Carper didn't smile.

"Sorry. Go ahead."

"I know this lab inside and out. I know where the keys are held and where guards won't be looking. It won't be easy to get out of here, but I think we have a chance. Problem is, it might take a while."

"You talk'n a couple days?"

"More like weeks."

I groaned and fought back the tears that stung my eyes.

"Try to memorize their patterns, when the guards leave and stay. I'll make Rose think I'm committed to doing what he says, which leads me to the next part."

"There's more?"

"Rose will expect me to experiment on you, like I did to your mom."

I gulped. "And what does that involve exactly?"

"Drawing your blood. I'll control it so that you don't lose too much at a time. At some point, I'll also have you take the plants."

I stood. "What? No. You can draw a little blood from me, but I'm not taking any plants. Those things turn people into monsters."

"You'll be able to fly."

"I don't care if they'll turn my skin to gold. If I eat those plants, there goes my chance of being coherent enough to remember I have a family waiting for me." This time, the tears fell. I turned my back and fixated on a florescent light blinking.

"Maybe..." Carper sighed. "Maybe you can pretend to eat the plants. I don't expect to see much results from your bloodwork anyway since you're not genetically related to Bahar."

I ran my fingers through my hair. "This sucks."

"Big time. Good news is I'm on your side."

I snorted. "How long this time?"

"If I actually listen to Elohim's warnings, you can count on it being forever."

Trudging toward the cot, I sat, then laid down, adjusting until I could settle as comfortably as possible. "I'm counting on it, Calvin."

Carper laid on his cot. He looked up at the ceiling.

I followed, returning my gaze to the blinking, dim light. "Why'd you do it?"

"Why did I betray you?"

"Yeah."

A couple beats followed. "I don't know. Pride, I guess."

It made sense. Didn't pride come before a fall? Imprisoned in his own cell was a pretty big fall.

"Pero?"

"Yep."

"You should be a king someday."

"Can't, silly. I'm a girl."

"A leader. You'd make a great Shea."

I smiled. "What about a Shua?"

"You'd make a great Shua, too."

Even without the confidence that we'd get out, I had a friend to hope for both of us. "Dr. Calvin Carper?"

"Yes, little girl who's not little."

"Thank you."

At least a minute passed in silence.

When I began to think he'd never reply, Carper cleared his throat. "You're welcome."

My smile broadened. Closing my eyes, I nearly drifted when a low and beautiful voice sang out.

This time, it was Carper's.

"You called me. You chose me.
   I am yours.
   All honor, all power, all battles are Yours.
   The battle is Yours."

He sang through the chorus once, and the second time through, I joined.

"I surrender all to You.
   Whoever You want me to be, I will be.
   Across the street, across the seas—
   whatever You want me to do I will do."

It was quiet after that. My soul felt full; my heart awakened. Our songs did not bring me visions. Elohim was our vision. I prayed that He'd continue to be for the many cold nights to come.

25

爱

Hours blurred, becoming days which turned to weeks of torture.

Just as Carper had predicted, Rose insisted I be experimented on. He called me Phase 1. Phase 2 would include Mom and Sam...whenever he found them. It was never clear what he'd do with our blood, except that he anticipated it'd make him the richest man on earth. If anyone knew the consequences that came with status and wealth, it was Carper. Still, Rose dedicated his days in a dark dungeon, believing he'd see his dreams of power fulfilled.

Each day, Carper would take my blood—not too much at a time—and use it to find out what I was good for. So far, nothing.

Every night, Carper would burst into songs that he'd learned as a Lesarie growing up. I caught on quickly, and we became a terrific duet. Rose gave us newly washed blankets because he said our skin now had a white tint. The white was more likely from lack of Vitamin-D and because I was already pale before I had blood taken out of me, but I wasn't about to complain.

When I wasn't playing guinea pig, I was allowed to roam the lab, which took exactly seven minutes and two seconds if walking swiftly. Most days, I felt like a caged animal pacing, my trainers ready to strike me with a whip at any sudden movement. The guards never hurt me, though. More than likely Rose saw me as too valuable to be tampered with. I'd let him keep thinking that.

The whole inside of the building screamed dreary, with cement walls and single hanging bulbs. The cement ceiling resembled a cave. The musty, damp smell reminded me that we really were under ground. Guards stood on a second story balcony that stretched around the entire premise and overlooked the open space below. On the catwalk, double doors led to Rose's headquarters where I'm sure he planned how to get rid of me if my blood proved to be normal. Adjacent to headquarters were the stairs leading into the emperor's palace. As I walked, I'd sometimes pause and look up with an ache in my chest. Was Henry alive? Had the sanctuary left without me? I hoped they had so they could be safe with the Lesaries in Origo. Were my parents looking for me or had they given up?

To the right of the courtyard, Carper's lab room brightened like Christmas lights. Clear windows surrounded the entire room, bringing the only source of bright light in a graveyard.

Inside Carper's lab, I wiggled in a dental chair, averting my eyes as Carper poked the needle into my skin. I grimaced. "You'd think I'd be used to this by now."

"I wonder how you survived me torturing you in Moon City, but you can't tolerate a little prick."

"Anticipation, I guess."

Carper put a cotton swab on my arm and wrapped it with an elastic strap. "Done."

I examined my arm, now covered with at least a dozen punctures. I laid my head back. "Any results?"

Carper took the vial to the counter and placed it in a holder. "I found one thing."

I lifted my head. "You did?"

"Don't get too excited. You're completely normal."

I laid my head back again and found my favorite spot on the ceiling. "Are you surprised?"

"A little. I expected to at least find abnormal functioning."

"Ha. I bet you would if you tested yourself."

The sound of clinking glass and pouring liquid warned me to keep my eyes glued to the ceiling. I'd watched once as he'd dripped my blood onto petri dishes to place under the microscope. Once was enough for my stomach to churn and vow to never look again.

"Anything new on your walk?" Carper asked.

"Two drops of water hit my head from the ceiling, but no indicator that a guard will fall asleep or leave his station for us to escape. They're not slackers, that's for sure."

Carper sighed. "I think Rose might be catching on that I'm not finding anything. Only a few more days at the most before he understands that 'Pero's blood shows promise' is a bunch of BS."

"Bad Science?" I grinned.

"Bad Subject."

"That's me." I grabbed a piece of hair and twirled, an old habit I'd somehow picked up again since being in Rose's prison. "Speaking of bad subjects, what do you think of this big party Rose is planning tomorrow? I still don't understand how it's a party with the three of us and a bunch of guards. Sounds sick, and not in a good way."

"I think he has a plan up his sleeve. Rose never hosts a party if there aren't enough people to make him look good."

"Reminds me of a man I used to know." I yawned. "Can't believe you forced me into that ridiculously fluffy dress."

"I had bad taste then. What can I say?"

"Think I'll have to wear a dress this time?"

"Most likely."

I closed my eyes and folded my arms. "I could totally fall asleep now. This chair is far more comfortable than that squeak'n cot."

"I slept on the ground last night instead."

I squinted one eye open and lifted my head to look at him. "Any better?"

"Not any worse." Carper stretched his neck to the left and right. "Although this kink is a pain in the neck."

"You sure that's from you sleeping funny or is it because you're—"

"Don't say it!"

"What'd you think I was going to say?"

"Something involving the letters O-L-D."

"That's not at all what I was thinking. I was going to say you're young and classy."

"Admit it, *xīn gān bǎo bèi*. I'm an old man."

I sat up slowly. "What'd you just call me?"

"Pero." Carper flushed, then turned back to his work. "I called you Pero."

"I've heard you call Cherry that. Does it mean daughter?"

"It essentially means *king of my world* or *dear to my heart*, a term parents often speak to their children. Now, let's drop it."

I scanned the lab with fresh eyes. Cherry grew up needing to stay with her father in his lab. But Carper wouldn't have treated her well. More than likely, she acted like his servant, waiting for his command or else she'd have to face his wrath. Was she dear to her father's heart?

"Did you experiment on Cherry?" My tone edged with rage. I couldn't understand why I choked back tears. Perhaps it was the reality that this same room wasn't a refuge for Mom or Cherry where they'd be safe from harm. This room represented pain.

Carper and I didn't waiver from our stare, until he finally broke the silence with a nod.

The girls who last sat in this chair were afraid and lonely with no way to escape their monster. I was his replacement, his daughter. The one who had no inhibitions when being in his company, while Cherry's childhood had been destroyed to please Carper. It wasn't fair.

Standing up, I headed to the door. "I need a moment."

Carper watched me walk away, a pained expression on his face that I refused to allow me feel anything but disdain.

THIRTY MINUTES LATER, Carper found me in my cell, laying on the cot and twirling my hair. He entered his cell—both of which were open during the day—and his cot squeaked as he sat. "Wanna talk?"

"Not really."

Silence answered, until Carper rose from his cot and started to leave.

"Wait." I sat up.

Carper kept his back turned, his ear leaning forward.

"Was Cherry ever dear to your heart?"

His shoulders sagged.

"Or did you not want anything to do with her the moment she was born?"

"I loved her."

"Then why did you shut her out? Why did you close yourself to anyone?"

Carper rubbed his head with his hands, then swiveled. "Part of me died the day they took my mother from me. She would be ashamed of who I became. She loved fiercely, while I loved by pushing her away. I didn't want her to learn from me, to be me. Instead, a part of my own daughter died when I shut her out." Carper trudged back over to the cot and sat in the middle. "Instead of facing my mistakes and making them right, I turned into a monster. Bitter. Angry. It was easier for me to kill the world rather than face it."

Nearly his whole life, Carper wore a mask, and Elohim had taken it off to reveal a hurt and lonely man with a wicked heart now surrendered into repentance. We all wore masks. Mine looked different than Carper's, but I still worked on peeling the pieces that remained glued onto my face: the pain of knowing I was left as a baby, the frustration that I didn't know how to fully love, the fear that I would be left alone again. Elohim had healed, yes, but those bits were hard to remove.

"I understand, in a way. You love Cherry, but you don't know how to mend what's been broken."

Carper placed his chin on his hands and rested his elbows on his knees. "Cherry can't forgive me. Maybe not ever. And she doesn't trust me." Carper laughed under his breath. "I don't blame her. I don't know if I can trust myself."

"I think she'll learn to forgive, but there will be days when she won't."

"She's a grown woman and has had a lot of years to hate me. But then you showed up..." Carper sniffled.

I sat on the edge of my cot so that I could be face-to-face. "Are you gonna cry?"

"No." Carper cleared his throat. "I never cry."

"So not true." My smile faded when his face stayed downcast. "You alright?"

"I'm not used to all this..." He waived his hand as if it'd help him find the right word. "...sentimental stuff. What I'm trying to say is that you showed up, and you were sassy and annoying, and I really did not want to deal with a teen girl, not when you reminded me of my own daughter. I tried to get you out of my life too, but then you had to be nice and save my life and

Elohim did something to my insides. Not like my organs or anything like that."

"I get it." I grinned.

"I'm not making any sense, so I'll get to the point. Pero, I accidentally called you *dear to my heart* or *king of my world* as I would've to Cherry because it's what I've been thinking about since Mr. Rose first tried to hurt you. I wanted to defend you, like a father. Maybe Elohim brought you to me for a second chance to be a good kind of father. This is going to sound cheesy, Pero, but for the first time in my life, I think I've learned what it means to love."

I let tears pour from my face without embarrassment. He was far from perfect, and he could use a Lesarie 101 class, if there was such a thing. But he cared.

In that moment, it became clear where I was supposed to be. Not be in love with Henry or Sam, nor seeking a love from a mother who sang to me but who still remained a mystery. And although my parents loved me, they were too far from reach, like more arms reaching for me but never fully holding.

Right then, for a season, I was to be loved by a God who wanted to be my Father and a man who chose to represent that fatherly love.

Carper wiped his own tears from his face. "I can't believe I said all that. I'm not planning on adopting you or anything like that. You have your parents, and I'm sure we'll see them again. And you don't have to accept anything I'm saying either. I'm okay if you never want to talk to me again."

I blinked back tears. "I might not be calling you *daddy* anytime soon, but of course I'll talk to you."

Carper looked around the room. "There might be a fly or two, but I might be your only choice."

"I *want* to talk to you. I am your adopted daughter, after all."

Carper returned my smile. "This is the first Hallmark

moment of my life." He stood tall. "And even though I meant everything I said, it will be my last."

I stood too, raising my chin. "Of course. Men must keep their dignity."

"You sound like some dead poet."

"Aw. Dr. Carper is back."

"Disappointed?"

"Relieved."

"Me too." He motioned for the cot. "Take that nap you wanted, if you can. I'm going to pretend I'm busy at the lab before Rose finds me missing."

I nodded, then yawned, drifting to sleep faster than I had in weeks.

26

相信

Aguard let me into the washroom, a small space with a lamp and incense on a side-table and a cracked full-length mirror. A tub filled with fresh water sat in the middle. A toilet was against the wall behind the tub.

"That toilet makes this my favorite room."

The guard grunted.

Every day in that miserable place, I used a bucket in my cell or, in another more private room, a squatty potty where I had to place a foot on either side of a trough. No toilet paper. On Saturdays, a guard let me into the washroom for a warm bath. Scrubbing myself clean was nice, but the perk was the toilet. I'd never been so excited to sit down while doing my business.

The guard pointed to a Chinese traditional dress hanging on the wall as well as the small table. "You wear." He bowed his head and left, closing the heavy door behind him.

There it was. The chosen dress for Rose's party. It appeared very traditional, like what I imagined Chinese princesses would've worn. It was a midnight blue satin with white delicate flowers swirling around. The sleeves were capped and trimmed in white. Round, satin buttons crossed from the side to the collar that appeared too snug around the neck. The beautiful silk was soft to touch.

At the small table—while looking for what the guard was pointing to that he wanted me to wear—I gasped. It was my necklace. I didn't think I'd see it again. The wooden feather felt both familiar and foreign under my touch. Wearing this necklace seemed like ages ago. That was when I thought it'd give me powers. Yet I'd still needed it for unlocking doors. I shuddered. Could it be the key for Carper and I to leave? Of course, Rose would've only given it to me if he wanted to use me for my powers at the party. He must've expected me to perform something spectacular.

As I removed my feet from the house slippers, a carving in the wooden wall made me pause. Someone had carved a symbol into the wall that looked identical to the word on the back of the pendant. I snatched the feather and turned it around. Yep. The same. *Koach*. Mom must've etched the word in this wall. Who else would've wanted the reminder that Elohim would be their strength?

Mom had been in this very room once when she was my age, perhaps looking into the same mirror, breathing in the sandalwood incense, washing in the metal tub, marveling over the luxury of a toilet.

I fingered the symbol in the wall. "Mom," I whispered. "I can't last here for years." I blinked before the tears that had pooled on my lashes escaped. "I'm not as strong as you."

Trust me.

"How much longer, Elohim? I thought you'd come after a day or two."

I removed my clothing, stepped into the tub, and sank into the water. The mildly warm temperature felt like needles pricking my skin. Goosebumps covered my flesh. I lathered the bar of soap that smelled of cedar and focused on something sticky on my foot, scrubbing until my skin felt raw. Still, the tar-like substance remained.

I threw the bar into the water. "See, Elohim? No matter how hard I try, the dirt never leaves. I'm stuck here. I'm sorry, but I'm having a hard time trusting you right now."

Give me the soap, and you will be clean.

I recalled when Yeshua led me to the river and washed my feet. He'd taken all the dirt away. Maybe the answer to escape wasn't searching for a flaw in the guards' stations or finding a door that the necklace could unlock; maybe I was to surrender.

"Okay, Elohim. Take the soap." I chuckled at the silly prayer, but trusting was better than wallowing in misery.

After washing my hair with fermented rice water, I climbed out of the tub, dried with a towel, then pulled the dress over my head. It landed just above my feet. Looking in the full-length mirror, I shook my head. The fabric tightened, emphasizing my flat stomach, tiny hips, thin legs. They fed me here, but Dad was right when he said I'd lost too much weight.

Running my hand down the side, I noticed a slit stopping at my upper-thigh. I cringed. The dress covered well enough if I stayed in one place, and at least I could move easier with the slit.

Picking up the brush someone had left for me on the small table, I worked through the tangles and tied it into a knot at the base of my neck. My eyes were sunken in from lack of sleep and my body resembled a stick figure, but I felt pretty.

Putting on the necklace, I tightened the pendant in my fist.

Mom.

A few months earlier, while prepping for Carper's party in his mansion, Mom came and brushed my hair and hugged me. My chest ached. She wouldn't be coming to rescue me again.

Would anyone?

THEY WERE LOST. Not literally. I later learned there were 192 people at the party in total, all between the ages of 13 to 20. It was their faces that told me they were lost, confused, out of place and out of reality. As if they were from another world.

The Chinese pop music blaring over the speakers and the cast of strobe lights in loud pinks and greens promised a raging party, but the chance of participation wasn't happening. People clustered in groups, watching each other and perusing the courtyard, sipping on drinks, girls tugging on their Chinese dresses, guys adjusting their ties. No one talked or laughed or smiled.

Who were these people, and where had Rose found them?

No sign of Rose yet. I spotted Carper hiding in the shadows and glided along the edge of the crowd in short, small steps.

Carper noticed me and met me in the middle. His eyes still lingered on the crowd as if he feared they'd jump him. "Couldn't find something to wear underneath that *qipao*?"

I straightened my legs so the slit was hidden. "I'm feeling self-conscious enough without you pointing it out."

"Sorry. Just feeling uptight."

"Figured." I followed Carper's lead and crossed my arms. "If Rose wanted me to hang with people my own age, he could've let me out. Far more seventeen-year-olds in Beijing than in here. Not to be rude, but this crowd doesn't seem ready for a boujee bash."

Carper raised his brows.

"It's a gen-z thing."

He nodded once, a scowl still on his face. "They don't recognize me, otherwise I'd be slaughtered."

"Who's 'they?'"

"The Warriors."

"Wait. You mean we're having a party with a bunch of dead people?"

"It appears they're still alive."

"Impossible. We both saw the walls crumble." I shivered at the memory of hundreds of dead bodies scattered underneath the debris.

"Either that or you and I died and are in…"

"You can say it. This place is hell."

Carper's face contorted as if in deep thought. "My guess is after we left Moon City, the ones who had still been taking the plants woke up. They were immortal as long as they ate them. And somehow, Rose found out they were alive and brought them here."

"So those who pretended to be taking the plants didn't make it."

"Right."

"And those who obeyed your ridiculous rule did."

"You got it."

"So unfair."

"Agreed."

"But the Warriors don't recognize you as their past dictator. Why?"

"When Moon City was destroyed, so were the gardens where the *li* grew. They had no choice but to return back to normal."

I took in the zombie-like crowd. "This isn't normal."

"That's because I took away their normalcy. They don't remember life without being drugged."

"Which also means they don't have the instinct to kill you right now. That's good news, Carper."

"Maybe. But I think Rose has an agenda, and I can't rest until I know what it is."

"Now's your chance to find out." I nudged my head toward our right where Rose stood in a grey suit and red tie. I'd never seen him smile so big.

Carper sucked in a breath and spoke through his teeth. "I'd rather dance with these zombies than talk with that son of a…"

"He's coming this way. Better get on the dance floor. Some-body's got to."

"And be recognized by my ex-warriors? No thanks."

I grabbed Carper's hand and pulled him into the middle of the crowd. "The best way to get rid of Rose is to dance. I know this from experience and a real dew-dropper named Jace."

Just as expected, Rose stopped mid stride and watched us.

"I don't dance." Carper stopped when we reached the middle. So did the crowd, waiting for us to do something. They'd probably never danced in their lives.

"You mean one of your many girlfriends didn't teach you how?" I swayed back and forth to the beat.

"Not the kind appropriate for your eyes."

I crinkled my nose. "Didn't need to know that."

The song changed to an upbeat classic.

"Hey!" I clapped my hands. "I know the choreography to this song. Learned it at school."

"Footloose was around when I was a teen, which makes me sound the word I can't get myself to say." Carper grinned. "I think I can remember the routine. Let's grab everyone's atten-tion to keep Rose out of the way."

I took off the house slippers and threw them to the side. "I'll do my best in this dumb dress."

Carper took off his suit jacket and handed it to me. "If it helps you feel more comfortable, you could tie this around your waist."

"I feel awkward either way, but I'll take it." I wrapped the jacket around my hips and made a double knot. "Much better. Thank you."

"It might help you move without looking like a penguin."

I laughed "You and Cherry are more alike than you realize."

"Tell me what you mean by that later."

We fell into step to the song. For a moment, I could block out the pain and pretend I was home. Back to the last school dance when the junior class spread across the gym and performed these exact moves: vine right, vine left, swivel heels. It was a simpler time, when the biggest thing I had to worry about was falling on my face in front of everyone and the hardest decision was whether to eat the safer cafeteria food choice of PB&J or risk the burrito.

Carper and I were synced. When Carper gave a spin in-between a hitch, a Warrior in the crowd hollered. More cheers followed. One ran into line with us and picked up the moves. Another joined, then more until around twenty were kicking off their Sunday slippers.

I didn't care about Rose. No one person could stop a group of this size. We could shake up the world one diagonal step at a time.

A girl in line next to me looked me in the eye and flashed a genuine smile. I smiled back, then did a double take and stopped. Didn't I know her from somewhere? She turned back to focusing on her feet, so it was difficult for me to study her face. Her bright red hair hung above her shoulders in elegant waves. Freckles by the millions adorned her otherwise porcelain skin. She was beautiful and graceful, could be a model on a runway. And so familiar.

Carper bumped into my elbow. I rubbed it with my hand.

"Sorry." Carper paused. "Why'd you stop? It's the best part."

I shook my head, watching as the red-headed girl walked away through the crowd. "Nothing. Thought I saw someone I knew."

"You could have seen any of these faces in Moon City."

"You're right." I smiled at Carper, then finished the last few steps before the song ended.

The Warriors clapped and hollered. Yep. Dancing solved just about everything, including waking up robotic teens. Nearly everyone mingled and laughed. Some began to dance again when the next song started.

Rose caught up to Carper. "A word?"

"Must we?" Carper put on a fake smile. "I was enjoying myself."

Rose scowled. "You're not fifteen any more, Carper."

"You sure about that?" Carper winked at me. "Fine then. If you must ruin my fun, where do you want to talk?"

"Your lab." Rose swiftly turned. "Now."

Good luck, I mouthed to Carper.

Thanks, he said.

At least I was off the hook this time. After I made sure Rose really took Carper to the lab and not the cell to be tortured, I swiveled and noticed that beyond the dance floor, the red-headed girl hovered in the shadow of a pillar. Her eyes stayed on me. She beckoned me to approach her with a small wave of her hand before disappearing behind the pillar.

The guards gazed straight ahead and not to anyone in particular. I crept through the crowd and toward the pillar, my quick-beating heart sounding a lot like hope.

"WHO ARE YOU?"

The pillar was large enough for both of us to hide from view. Still, she looked like a deer in the headlights, her head darting back and forth to make sure no one listened in. Her hair crashed over her delicate face as she leaned near my ear. "It's me, Cathena."

My head throbbed, cascading down my body. "It can't be you. The Cathena I met this summer was much younger and not so...sophisticated."

"Being on the plants stunted my growth. I'm eighteen. And time is slower here than in Origo." Her mousy voice confirmed her identity. It was deeper but still resembled an operatic soprano.

"So I've been told." Shea must've been ancient at that point.

A crash from above us had us both jumping. I glanced upward and spotted guards trading post positions. Must've been a door slamming shut.

"We need to leave." Cathena looked around again and whispered so low I could barely understand. "I have a plan."

"A plan?"

"Shh."

Heat traveled up my neck. "Sorry."

"Tonight. Be ready." Cathena hesitated, then focused solely on my eyes. "Henry's alive." She took a final glance around her, then stepped onto the dance floor, joining the Warriors in the weirdest moves I'd ever seen. Was that supposed to be break dancing? Looked more like twitching to hold a full bladder.

I shook my head to clear my thoughts. Cathena was here. For real! I didn't know how she'd pull off an escape, but she seemed confident. And so mature. I still couldn't get over the fact that she looked grown up and was older than me.

She said Henry was alive. How did she know unless she'd been outside first? What did she mean by tonight? I needed to tell Carper. Stepping around the pillar and to the clearing, I looked for Carper and Rose through the glass wall of the lab. They were gone.

Panic drummed through me like a spastic heartbeat. Where had Rose taken Carper? Weaving my way through the crowd, I peeked into the open door of the lab. Yep. Gone. I swallowed a lump in my throat and sped to the open archway that led to the cells. Guards turned their heads to watch me but did nothing to stop my hustle. They didn't seem to care where I went, as long as I didn't head for the exit.

My dread increased as I hurried through the empty, dank hall and through another archway into the prison. It was dark inside except for the blinking light that had nearly brought me to insanity on more than one sleepless night. It was quiet.

I turned on my heel, then stopped when I heard a groan coming from a cell.

"Carper?" I ran over and found him lying on the ground on his back, one side of his body against the bars and inside the cell. When I pulled at the cell's door, it didn't budge. *No!* I knelt on the ground and reached an arm between the bars until my hand met his shoulder. "What did he do to you? Thank Elohim you're alive."

"Barely." Carper choked out the word.

"You can speak. That's a good sign."

Carper turned his head slowly. "Any sign of blood?"

I patted his head. "Hard to see, but I don't feel any. From what I can tell, your cheek is swollen. And right after you recovered from your last blow. Your poor face will never be the same."

"Perfect faces are overrated." Carper grimaced as if it hurt to talk. "Turns out Rose likes punches. Better than bullets."

I kept a hand on his arm, hoping it'd give him some comfort. "Can you sit up?"

"I feel a little dizzy so am going to stay here a bit longer."

"I can get you a drink."

Carper shook his head. "Don't trust Rose's party drinks."

"I had some water, haven't fallen over yet."

"Fine. But only if you're careful. I don't want you near Rose."

Sounded like a fair bargain to me. "What made him angry this time?"

"He called my bluff. Decided he's going to give me 24 hours to make some potion that will return the Warrior's powers or he'll kill us both. He must have scientists confused with wizards. And the Warriors have no clue. It's like they woke up from hibernating and don't understand what's right or wrong in this situation. They'll just go with the flow. The point is, we're dead."

"You think Rose means it this time?"

Carper blew out a long breath. "Probably."

Water dropping from the ceiling counted the seconds of silence. Drip, drip, drip. Time would soon be gone.

"Cathena's here." I forced a smile, hoping it would bring some encouragement. "She has a plan."

Carper chuckled. "Stone was always the most fierce and skilled of the Warriors. Maybe we stand a chance."

"I think she's the answer to our prayers."

"Hope you're right, Pero." Carper sat up slowly with a grunt and leaned against the bars. "Now where's that drug-free water you promised?"

"Right away, *Bàba*." I stood.

Carper looked up at me. "You called me 'dad.'"

He was the closest I had to family right now, and perhaps for a very long time. We needed each other to survive. I shrugged. "Seemed fitting since you were bossing me around."

"The best parents do."

"Then you must be one of the best."

27

———

救援

As soon as I entered the party room, Rose approached me.

"There you are." He grabbed my wrist and squeezed.

I held back the tears that stung my eyes.

"I need you to sing."

"Like right now?"

"How else am I going to test your power?" He pushed me up one step onto a small platform and handed me a mic. "I didn't give you back your necklace for nothing."

I touched the pendant, now heavy against my chest. "I'll sing on one condition."

Rose raised a brow.

"If a door opens, you'll let me and Carper go."

Rose smirked. "No one's going through a door if it opens."

"Then why test my powers?"

"I need to know the depths of your ability."

"Sorry to disappoint you, Mr. Rose, but what you see is what you get."

With an intense glare, Rose grabbed the mic from my grasp

and pressed his phone's screen with the other hand. The music stopped, as did the party.

"May I have your attention?" Rose's voice boomed like thunder.

The Warriors straightened, more than likely subconsciously recalling the stiff posture they stood in every day for years.

"Thank you for coming to my party."

I resisted an eye roll. As if they had a choice.

"You can call me Mr. Rose. I know you've all had a long journey, and you more than likely wonder what you're doing here in a lab under the Forbidden City, the heart of China. But I want to bring you hope."

Yeah, right.

"Starting tonight, your lives will change for the better. A famous scientist is in the process of developing a plant that will make you indispensable. When you came from the other world, you were afraid and alone. This plant will make you stronger, faster, younger. You will live forever."

Okay, even if Carper could develop a plant that powerful, I doubted he could do it in twenty-four hours.

Rose lifted his head as if in triumph. "The entire country and eventually the world will know that you are the heart of China. I call you The Warriors."

I did roll my eyes at that point. *So original.*

"Tomorrow you will start eating this plant, but for now I want us to see a taste of this power. It is in the voice of an angel." Rose swept his arm out in a grand gesture. "I give you Pero."

No one applauded.

Rose handed me the mic and clapped loudly as he headed off the platform. It echoed in the silent room until he finally stopped.

"Thanks for the warm introduction," I said into the mic.

I didn't even get a smile.

Clearing my throat, I motioned to Rose who approached me. "What am I supposed to sing?"

"You tell me. You're the one with powers." Rose stepped back.

I wasn't about to explain that any power I received was really Elohim's. Rolling my shoulders back, I lifted the mic, feeling naked without my guitar. I'd sing what Carper taught me in the cells and that we'd sung every night since.

"You called me. You chose me."

The Warriors perked, leaning forward as if it was the first song they'd ever heard. Maybe it was.

"I am yours."

I closed my eyes as tears gathered behind them. Why cry now? I'd heard this song dozens of times, and never had it moved me as much as I sensed it did now. When I opened my mouth, intense beauty flowed out, just like an angel as Rose had commented. I'd always known the sound of my voice but perhaps never really heard it for who it represented.

Pero Ruth Moshe, hidden in her Creator: pure, strong, lovely.

No vision flashed before me. Doors didn't open. Light didn't appear. A woman didn't sing a lullaby.

But He came.

Elohim's presence in the room felt like sinking into a bed of feathers. Thick, yet oh so light.

The need to cry turned into an urgency to laugh. It started with a small smile on my lips, followed by a chuckle, which then grew to an eruption of giggles. I pulled the mic away, threw my head back, and laughed like a child. Free. Secure. Unrestrained.

Kneeling to the ground and hunching over, I dropped the mic, joy like sparklers setting my heart on fire. It didn't feel like hysterics, more like a battle where Rose was the enemy, Elohim the hero, and laughter the greatest weapon of all. Whatever the reason, I embraced it. I'd laugh in evil's face. I'd dismiss torture's call. As the daughter of a powerful King, I chose life when the walls didn't crumble.

One of the Warriors snickered, which like a spark igniting into a blazing flame, brought them all into fits of laughter.

I lifted my hands to the sky—beyond the walls and ground that closed me in—and sang out again, this time fuller and with a reason to praise.

"I surrender all to You. Whoever You want me to be, I will be."

"Enough!"

The laughter ceased.

Through the tears that clouded my vision, Rose's feet lingered where I crouched. Trying to hold it in, I snorted.

"Up!"

After a small lift, I sat back down. "It's really difficult to do that in this dress."

Rose clenched the dress on my back and pulled. A rip sounded, and a draft moved beneath my left armpit.

I stood carefully and examined the rip. A piece of fabric hung open, revealing a few inches of my side. "Can I go back to my cell?"

Rose took my arm and yanked me close. "You've had enough time with Carper, don't you think? Wouldn't want you to be making *plans*."

My gaze flitted to his, then away. Did he overhear me and Carper or Cathena? Did Cathena really have a plan? I glanced at the room before looking down again. Wouldn't want Rose to think I was searching for someone.

"She's not here anymore. We made sure of that."

I frowned. "Who's not here?"

Rose's grip around my wrist tightened. "You think I don't see anything. The gig with Cathena is over, and so is your performance."

My body trembled. I willed my face to stay neutral, but the twitch in my cheek didn't help. "What gig?"

He faced the crowd. "Party's over." At the wave of his hand, guards assembled the Warriors, and they formed into a line, walking through a door to who knows where. Did they have more prison cells, or did the Warriors have luxurious rooms?

Rose turned back to me. "Don't play dumb, Pero."

Cathena hadn't told me the plans, but it appeared I was in trouble either way. The anxious tremble in my body turned to rage. "What'd you do to her?"

"Nothing that Carper hasn't done to her already."

My breathing shallowed, the joy that lingered only moments ago nowhere in sight. "He's different, you know."

Rose bellowed in laughter, causing some of the guards to turn heads before resuming their positions. Maybe the guards were heartless. How else would any decent human being stay immovable without a blink while a man contorted my arm as if it were made of rubber?

"Naïve little girl, a pawn in Carper's game."

I yanked away from his hold. "You don't know anything."

Rose sunk his fingers into my shoulder.

I grimaced, sure of the deep imprint it'd leave behind.

He pressed his lips to my ear, and I tried to pull away. "You think Carper's a saint, but he's just another man who won't stop until he gets what he wants."

Strength drained from my pores as if I was slowly melting. I wished I could. Then I wouldn't have to recognize the greed in Rose's gaze and the intentions in his grip.

Elohim, help!

The guards stayed at attention, nothing fazing their stoic stance. The last of the Warriors in line wandered from the room like lost sheep without a cause. No one came as Rose dragged me in the direction of his headquarters. Past the last strand of strength. Closing in on the end of hope.

MY FUTURE LAY BEFORE ME. Cathena was gone, Henry too. I'd be a slave forever. I willed my body to faint to avoid facing whatever was to come, but my racing heart kept me awake. Instead, as Rose threw me into his room and slammed the door behind us, I shut down. When the sound of a lock on the door clicked, I imagined holding a lever in hand and pulled the switch to one part of me at a time.

The mind—its fears and wonderings—off.

The body—blood rushing, stomach churning—off.

The soul and all its expectations—off.

Exist. Don't feel. Get through.

Believe in me.

Faith makes suffering too painful, Elohim.

Let me take your pain.

All things were at their end: happiness, innocence. Perhaps this was my fate.

Rose slapped my face.

I nearly crumbled from the impact. Placing my hand on my cheek, I staggered. The pain followed, a dull throb. No blood.

"That's for making me look a fool tonight." Rose drew closer, smothering, crowding.

I screamed out His name. "Elohim!"

Rose smirked. "Your God can't save you."

I closed my eyes to shut him out, then opened them briefly. No one stood behind Rose one second, but someone appeared the next. My eyes widened at the ghostly form of Cathena. She appeared like a hologram, body not fully present and scanning the room as if she couldn't see us.

Rose turned his head to where I stared, his body following. He saw the figure and scurried back, tripping and spilling to the floor. He took me back with him, one leg pinning mine.

"Guards!" Rose shouted.

I squirmed my leg from under his hold and punched him in the mouth. He staggered. I jumped to my feet. Rose tried to grab my leg, but I swerved around his reach and stepped on his hand, kicking him in the ribs.

He groaned and curled up on his side.

Cathena became fully present and with spear in hand, planted her feet. Her grey eyes hardened; her red hair appeared darker, as if lava consumed every strand, ready to erupt in vengeance.

Rose whimpered. "Please, don't. I won't hurt anyone. I promise—"

In one swift movement and a mighty roar, Cathena brought her arm back behind her head and thrust the spear forward. The tip plunged into Rose's stomach.

Rose convulsed. Blood poured from his gut and throat, followed by a soft gurgle, then silence. Rose's eyes stayed open, his body still.

I turned my head, trying to get my mind off of the bile that built in my throat.

A knock on the door sounded. A voice spoke in Chinese.

I swiveled to Cathena.

"You okay?"

I shook my head.

The knocking increased.

My eyes grew wide, muscles trembling so hard that I couldn't move.

Cathena kneeled near me, then reached out her hand. "Hold on."

Too stunned to speak or ask why, I nodded and placed my hand in hers.

And then the room was gone.

28

唱歌

A blink later, Cathena and I appeared in a softly lit room where Chinese gods lay scattered about in broken pieces. The red curtain was torn in two. We'd landed in the shrine.

I didn't care to ask how we teleported into another room. Right then, all I cared about was the man standing before me. I ran and plowed into Henry. He fell back a few steps before stabilizing us both. His arms around me felt supportive while mine around him were desperate, as if the slightest breath would fly me away if I dared to let go.

Clinging to him, I sobbed.

A moment later, he gently pulled me back. He knelt at eye level to ensure he had my full attention. "You're safe, Pero. Whatever happened is over."

Wiping the tears with the edge of my shirt, I took a deep breath and noticed a scar along Henry's head where he'd been injured. How was his injury already scarred? It had only been a few weeks. "He's gone. Rose is dead."

Henry nodded. "Home is a step away, and I'm going to get you there."

I sniffled. "What about Carper?"

Henry glanced at the red curtain. "He's waiting for us in the garden."

My jaw dropped. I stepped away from Henry, letting his hands fall to his sides. They got Carper out of there before me. Incredible. "And the Lesaries?"

"They are in Origo and are safe."

I paused mid-step, nearly crumbling with relief. They were safe, and soon we all would be. "I should find Carper. He'll be worried."

Henry placed a hand on my arm. "We need to talk first."

I turned and slid my gaze back to Cathena who watched me and waited. I'd nearly forgotten she was there. "Thank you for coming when you did." I nearly choked on the words. I'd been so close to more torture, a long life of it, really. And I'd given up all hope. Elohim had a plan all along, and I didn't believe it. I only could see what was right in front of me, while Elohim saw beyond.

Cathena approached me, wrapped her arms around me, and squeezed. "You were a good fighter yourself." Stepping back, she paused.

Something felt off. Words weren't being said. "What's going on?"

Cathena and Henry glanced at each other, then back to me.

"Pero." Cathena ran her fingers through her hair, looking like she returned from the salon rather than a battle. "After I got off of the plants, I began to notice something about me that was unusual. Rare, actually."

I scrunched my nose. "What is it?"

"I'm a transporter."

I glanced at Henry. "You both are transporters?"

"Yes." Henry spoke with hesitation, then swallowed hard.

I recalled Henry's words about transporters choosing to date or marry each other, that it made it easier for them. And here was Cathena, a grown and beautiful woman and a transporter. And Henry.

I took in his scar, thin and faded. Lines formed on his forehead, giving him a maturity that replaced his boyish charm. His hair was now at his shoulders and a darker blonde. A goatee outlined the shape of a beard. "Where did you jump from before you came here?"

He avoided looking at me for too long. "Origo." He gave a slight nod, as if begging that I'd understand.

I gulped. "For how long?"

"Two years."

I bit my trembling lip. "You couldn't find me for two years?"

Henry rubbed the back of his neck. "We tried. We thought you'd—"

"That I what, Henry?" I swatted a stray tear. "Died?"

Henry's throat bobbed up and down. "Elohim brought us here." He pointed to Cathena. "It was a total surprise, but we knew we'd find you this time. We missed you."

"We?" My voice squeaked.

Cathena cleared her throat. "I'll be waiting in the garden."

I kept my eyes on Henry as he watched her walk away. When he finally turned back to me, I straightened. "How long have you two been together?"

Henry rubbed his chin. "It's not like that, Pero. We're only friends. Besides, we shouldn't be talking like this right now. You just got out of a traumatic situation."

"Don't tell me what I got out of." The use of my first name instead of my nickname didn't escape me. I folded my arms. "How long?"

"For what?"

"That you've liked her."

Henry groaned. "I'm not going to answer that. Just because we're both transporters doesn't mean we're supposed to be together."

"I need to know."

"Why?"

Perhaps it was to settle what I'd sensed for a while now. Henry and I were not meant to be together. We never had the same relationship that I admired in Mom and Dad, with trust, teamwork, forgiveness. But my need to know was more than that. I longed to hear that I wasn't left by someone else and quickly forgotten.

Henry took a step closer. "Please, understand me. Two years is a long time. But don't forget that I loved you, Ro girl."

I shook my head. "I'm not your girl anymore."

"No, but you're somebody's. Elohim's crazy about you. Your parents have checked in with a search team every day. Shea and Jehoshua still believe you'll return. Cherry prays for you. Love isn't found in one person; it's shared with those Elohim brings into our lives. They didn't forget about you because love never gives up. They're waiting for you."

"What if they've all moved on?"

Henry's smirk revealed his dimple, the only remains of the guy I used to know. "Goodbye's not forever when it involves Pero Moshe."

I grinned.

Henry extended an arm. "Let's get you home."

I let out a shaky breath. "I'm nervous."

He looked me in the eye. "It's time, Pero."

I relaxed my tight muscles. "You're right, but we can't leave without the Warriors. The guards might torture them, and they deserve a second chance."

"You haven't changed."

"You have." I studied his chin. "What's that stuff on your face?"

"It's called facial hair."

"Aw! Henry's so grown up!"

He jabbed me. "Cathena will agree that we shouldn't leave the Warriors behind."

"Carper will, too."

Henry nodded. "Let's go save some Warrior booty."

I poked him in return, and my mouth lifted into a smile. If Henry didn't have feelings for Cathena now, it had to be coming. She was beautiful and a transporter. He'd be a fool not to fall in love with her. For now, I had my friend back. He was alive, and that was more than enough for me.

29

決定

The Warriors marched in a single line, filing out from under the ground and entering the emperor's room.

The four of us peeked from behind the entryway.

"Guess they didn't need to be rescued after all." I crouched low.

"It can't be that easy." Carper stood, his head looking above mine.

"Their leader is dead." Cathena glanced at Henry as if to make sure he was still near. He was very near for just a friend, and her flushed cheeks and bright eyes confirmed Cathena welcomed the close proximity. So, maybe *she* had a thing for *him*.

Henry's eyes shifted to me, and I turned away.

"It appears the guards could care less about keeping them hostage," Cathena continued. "Maybe there was money involved when Rose was alive. Without him around, no payment."

"Good point," Carper said. "People do anything for money."

I scrutinized his face, and he answered with a remorseful expression.

When the Warriors all had left the exit, a guard pointed at the rest of the palace and spoke in Mandarin.

"He said they needed to leave."

The Warriors paused with uncertainty.

"They don't know where to go." Without a leader, they were free, but what did independence mean to one who'd never been taken off the leash?

Henry pulled away. "I'll get them settled. They can stay in the sanctuary. It's all open now, so there won't be any reason to hide, and the space is available for use with the Lesaries gone. At least, it has been for a couple of years."

I lifted myself from the crouched position. "I'll help you."

Henry shook his head. "As much as I'd love the help, Pero, the best place for you to be is home."

The word "home" tugged at my heartstring, and I knew in that moment, returning to my family was the right thing to do. They waited for me, and I for them.

I nodded in agreement. "Will you stay, Cathena?"

She glanced at Henry. "Maybe for a bit, until the Warriors settle. Then I'll be back while Henry's busy in medical school."

My head jerked. "You're going to medical school?"

He pushed back his hair. "I'll never forget when you told me I'd be a good doctor someday."

I grinned. "I can't believe you're making it happen. What school?"

Henry pointed behind him. "Here, actually. In Beijing. I'm going to study traditional Chinese medicine."

The smile spread. "I'm proud of you."

He squirmed and averted his eyes. "Thanks. That means a lot."

Carper cleared his throat. "I'll be going back with Pero. No need for me to stay."

Henry nodded. "Makes sense."

An awkward pause followed. The Warriors trudged in the

other direction, where they'd walk through the Forbidden City's gates. They watched the premises as if searching for a sign that would make their next steps clear.

Henry glanced their way for a moment. "I better catch up to them before they take off into the city without a clue of where to go." He slapped his hands and rubbed them together. "I guess this is goodbye...for now."

I gulped. Would it be forever this time? In a way, Henry had already left the night he was taken in the back of an ambulance, my heart with it. Perhaps it was better this way, to watch him leave once again and live his happy life full of knowledge and purpose.

It was time for me to release him and find Elohim's purpose for my own life. Contentment fell slowly until it settled in my soul. Yes, I was okay to move forward and meet the promises of bright-filled days.

Cathena approached me, gave my arm a gentle squeeze. "When I return, I...I'd like to be friends."

I hugged her. "I'd like that." And I meant it.

Cathena smiled, said goodbye, and turned to give Carper a quick embrace. The two of them spoke in hushed tones.

I studied the ground, my house slippers, Henry's shoes, then finally his face.

He stepped forward and reached his arm out. "Come here." He tightened his grip for a moment, then let go. Too short. Like the couple of weeks we were together. "Bye, Ro."

I tried a smile, a single word, but nothing happened. I just stood there staring, as if I peered into the past and a pane of glass rested between us. Close yet ever so far.

Henry's brows drew together. "You gonna be okay?"

Still dumbfounded, I nodded.

His breath came out long as if he'd been holding it.

Cathena approached and touched his arm. "We should go."

He gave a small wave, then they both turned and walked away.

"Goodbye, Henry Beggs," I whispered.

Henry and Cathena approached the Warriors and led them into their first taste of freedom. Their stride was in unison, side-by-side. A small gesture that had always felt impossible between me and Henry.

"Should I find a wheelchair?"

I glanced at Carper right behind me. "What for?"

"You're as stiff as Anna in ice."

I swiveled. "Who's Anna?"

"Oh, come on! You know *Footloose* but not *Frozen*?" He brought his arm around my middle and walked me in the opposite way of Henry, the direction my body fought against but my mind knew was where I belonged.

Away from a palace, a deserted kingdom, a handsome grown man and his friend.

To the red curtain, the hidden garden, the sucky machine. To another universe and the people I loved.

It was time to come home.

30

幕

Was it the dim lighting from the setting sun or had the grass in the field turned brown? The trees too looked like they'd been scorched black by a fire, burnt and dead. What had happened here? Either it was the middle of winter or a fire had come through the meadow. But the cabin still stood in the distance, the same light from the window directing my steps forward.

Follow the light.

What was it about this place that brought such comfort? As if I'd finally discovered where I'd come. Or had I?

"Where are the Lesaries?" Carper asked. "Looks like we're the only ones here."

I turned down his question to a low simmer, not caring to answer, only to find what or who lay inside the cabin. The light drew me. A question waiting for my answer.

And then I heard the hum, gentle, caring.

The voice began to sing the familiar song. Whoever was inside, sang for me. I sensed it with every fiber of my being.

"I need to follow that light." I walked faster, and barely noticed when Carper sped up to match my pace.

"What's wrong with you? You're jumpier than if we'd landed on Mars."

I kept my eyes focused on the cabin ahead, the urge that someone I needed was in there becoming stronger with each step forward. "Not sure what it is about this area that feels safe. It's like I'm meant to land here, in-between wherever I'm heading to next."

"A resting place."

"I guess."

Carper tugged at my arm and stopped me mid-stride. I caught myself before falling forward.

"What do you think you'll find there, Pero?" His eyes narrowed, seeking mine as if he wanted me to examine my heart, then lay it bare.

I shook my head slowly. "Not 'what' but 'who'."

Carper's hand still held firmly to my arm. "Who will you find?"

A dozen possibilities swarmed in my head: my birth mom, Mom, Sam, perhaps an empty place that I could settle into. My gaze landed on the small cabin, the light pouring out like a spotlight pointed directly at…

"Me." I looked back to Carper. "I'll find myself."

"I didn't realize you were missing."

I took a deep breath. "It's not like that. I know who I am and what I want in life."

Carper lifted his chin a smidge. "You do?"

Crossing my arms, I fixated on a smudge on Carper's shoe. "I think so. I am who Elohim made me to be: funny, tenacious, curious."

"And a good friend." Carper winked.

The side of my mouth tilted.

"Keep going." Carper nudged his head. "What do you want in life?"

"I want to live." Lifting my head to the sky, I breathed in

crisp air, a contradiction from the burnt woods around us. I watched a flock of birds as they glided across the horizon that turned the clouds to a soft pink. Closing my eyes, I listened to the song, low and faded into the background of my mind.

"For so long, I thought I needed to grab opportunities as soon as they came. I longed for next week's dream to find me far from Green Meadow. Although being kidnapped wasn't what I had in mind, you made that happen." My eyes opened to see Carper attentive, expression fully engaged. "I wanted my mom to return, but mostly I craved change. Henry was my escape from feeling stuck. Sam was an obsession to distract me from pain. Well, more of a recognition of something unique between us. And my mom was a distant memory." I bit my lip. "I'm not closing myself off from love or friendship or family. I need you all. But I like being where I feel known by Elohim without the pressure to decide anything else."

"Then how does rushing to a cabin in the middle of nowhere help you find yourself?"

The voice that had sung to me for the last couple months came from that tiny cabin, the very place Mom's life had truly begun. "Because I was born there."

Carper glanced at the cabin, then back to me. "How do you know that?"

"Sam said so. The woman who took him in—Alexis—also cared for me before my mom—Bahar—took me to another world. Bahar picked up a baby lying in front of a tree in these very woods, and that baby's name was Ruth, which happens to be my middle name."

Carper's eyes widened. "Is Alexis your birth mom?"

Why hadn't I made that connection before? "Sam didn't mention if she is."

Carper tapped his fingers against his crossed arms. "You say the voice seems to be coming from this house."

"Correct. And the thought 'follow the light' has gone

through my brain a bajillion times. Not sure if that's Elohim or what, but I feel I'm supposed to be here."

"Well, why are you standing next to an aging scientist?" Carper nudged me forward. "I would've run there right away if I were you."

I willed my legs to move, but they wouldn't. My brain stuck on the word Carper said. *Run.* Why was I eager to run? To find my worth? I didn't need the knowledge of who birthed me to determine who I was. Neither my bio mom nor my adopted mom raised me. Dad had, and I'd been fine. Not perfect, but he'd loved me and kept me alive. Did I really need to follow the light?

"You're hesitating."

I lowered myself on the dry grass and crisscrossed my legs, thankful I'd found better clothes to change into before we traveled across universes. Breathing out a heavy sigh, I studied the smoke rising from the cabin's chimney. "I'm unsure if I want to meet her."

Carper sat next to me. "Ouch." He readjusted so that his legs were crisscrossed like mine. "This grass is as sharp as needles." He plucked a blade and twirled it between his fingers. "I wonder if a fire swept through here."

Tucking my legs in for a hug, I fought the growing agitation boiling through my blood. "I could care less about the ground right now."

Carper blew out a puff of air. "The answer is simple. Don't meet her."

I turned to him and glared.

"What? They were your words."

Hearing the humming once again, I looked back to the open window. "What if she's not there?"

"Could be the Lesaries waiting for you to hurry up and get inside so they can throw you a welcome home party. Not sure how they'd all fit in there."

I rolled my eyes.

"Bad time for humor. Got it." Carper cleared his throat. "Why are you hesitating, Pero?"

"Because I'm done running, and if finding the source of this voice is another one of my daily runs, I don't want it." My pulse rose, and I forced myself to breathe. "There are only so many times I can chase after the wind."

I listened to the crickets chirping for at least a minute before Carper spoke. "I see it differently."

A quick glance at Carper's contemplative face told me he'd thought this through.

"The question is, are you running ahead or away? If you're running out of fear or insecurities, then you should stay put. Or maybe you could check it out but choose not to let the answers define you. But if you're seeking something good, something that Elohim Himself may have put right in front of you, then it'd be ridiculous to sit here and do nothing."

Setting my face in my hands, I rubbed hard. He was right. And perhaps that's what Jehoshua meant when he said to stop running. Maybe instead of looking for a way out, I needed to look for a way forward.

I stood, wiped the dust from off my legs, and squared my shoulders.

"I'll stay a distance behind you." Carper got to his feet. "But I should go with you, just to make sure it's safe."

I nodded, gaze still set ahead.

Carper placed a hand on my shoulder. "Go get her."

I took off on a race that my heart decided would make me a winner, no matter the prize.

31

住

My hand hovered over the solid wood for a moment before I knocked on the same door that had led Mom to her destiny, the same door that Sam's dad —Salmon—had formed with his own hands. Built out of faith and obedience, without the knowledge that it'd create such a moment as this.

Anticipation fluttered in my stomach. The door opened slowly and Alexis peeked through, brightened, and opened it wide.

"Pero! What are you doing here? Come in."

I froze. What if I was wrong and this was all in my head?

"Is something wrong?" Alexis asked. "Is it Sam?"

I shook my head.

Relief flooded her face. She walked inside, leaving the door open for me to come when ready. I glanced behind me to find Carper giving me the thumbs up, then walking away. I turned back to the threshold, peering inside to an open space with a cozy fire that crackled sparks, a small kitchen to the left, two lonely chairs to the right. Ahead, one door was left ajar to what I assumed was a bedroom. I inhaled the yeasty smell of loaves that spread across the counter, exhaled the fear of disappointment that I'd reached a dead end.

Alexis fluttered about the kitchen, placing a pan in the sink, taking a glimpse at another batch in the oven. If she noticed I hadn't moved, she didn't say anything.

"Sam's living in the younger universe now." She plopped a ball of dough onto a flour-coated counter and dug her fist in to kneed. "And the Lesaries are sweeping through any time now. They wanted to gather water and supplies before coming this way, and I wanted to make enough bread to feed a multitude."

Pulling my heavy feet inside, I closed the door behind me and took a better look around. Beautiful cedar adorned the walls, appearing smooth and durable, like the work of a skilled carpenter. Sam's dad had built these walls and kept Mom safe, and now the same walls held this woman near me. I took in her features. Long and wavy hair, silver with hints of chestnut. Exotic brown eyes with slight crinkles on the side. Skin the color of honey. I searched for clues that I was her Ruth, but felt all possibilities slip into a coma. Like my body did. Limp. Asleep. Refusing to rush to conclusions.

"Are you sure you're okay?" She poured a cup of tea, handed it over, and pulled out a chair. "Sit. You look pale. And filthy. I'll get a bath started." Alexis picked up a tea kettle from the stovetop. "You should have time before the Lesaries come, and then you can tell me all about your latest adventures."

My numb mind somehow told my body to sit. After taking a sip, I set the cup that Sam had probably carved onto the soft wood floor. "Did you ever find Ruth?"

Alexis swiveled, the smile from her lips fading. She placed the kettle on the stovetop, turned on the burner, then lowered herself into the chair next to me. "Sam told you?"

"A little." Too hard to explain that I'd been here not too long ago when younger Mom had taken the baby away. She wouldn't remember such a crazy time warp or that I saw a scene of my younger self right before my eyes.

Grabbing a piece of hair to twirl, I bit my lip, considering my next words. She wouldn't tell me the back story without me asking, and I needed more evidence before knowing if she really was my birth mom. "What—happened?"

Alexis sighed. "Ruth was taken by a woman one day. I don't think she knew the baby would disappear with her. No one did."

"We're you…?" I swallowed. "Were you Ruth's mother?"

Alexis leaned back against her chair. "If you don't mind, I'd rather not talk about it."

"Then, who was Ruth's father?" I leaned forward. "Can you tell me that?"

Alexis raised a brow. "Why so curious all a sudden?"

"I need to find out if—"

A knock on the door made me jump in my seat.

Alexis rose and hurried to answer. "Did someone come with you?"

I rubbed my forehead. "Only Carper." Who had very bad timing.

When no noise followed, I lifted my head to find Alexis paused in front of the door, unmoving.

Another knock.

"Is something wrong?"

Alexis shook her head. "Nothing." She placed a hand on the knob, shuddered, then opened.

Carper didn't seem to notice that Alexis' face had turned a shade pink and her hands began to tremble.

"Sorry to interrupt." Carper perused the cabin, then looked to me and Alexis. "You must be Alexis. I never had the chance to meet you at the Lesaries' camp last time I was here, but I had your food. The best chili I've ever had."

He offered her a hand, and she hesitated, then shook for a millisecond before dropping her hand to her side.

"Thank you, Dr. Carper." She moved away from the door and appeared to move away from him as well. "Come on in."

Carper took a step forward. "Wanted to give you a heads up that the Lesaries are coming. Could see the storm of them from a mile away."

Alexis walked backward, nearly tripped on a chair, then straightened it before heading to the kitchen. "Guess you won't have time for a bath after all, Pero." As the kettle started its whistle, she clicked the knob on the stove to turn off the burner. "Would you like some tea, Dr. Carper?" Her voice was uneven. "Or maybe a slice of bread?"

Carper took the seat next to me. "No, thank you." He sniffed the air. "On second thought, I better take your offer before the Lesaries eat it all."

Alexis nodded her head, then stumbled her way through laying out a plate and a slice.

Carper leaned near my ear and whispered. "Did you find out?"

I folded my arms. "Was just about to."

Carper grimaced. "Is Alexis always this nervous?"

"Only when you walked in."

Carper straightened and with knit brows, fixated on the floor.

Alexis' hand shook, and tea sloshed out of the cup and onto the floor.

Carper rushed near her and accepted it from her hands. "Thank you." He also took the small wooden plate with two slices of steaming bread and placed it on the counter. "You can sit there."

With head down, Alexis sat in the chair and adjusted the fabric of her skirt that fell to her ankles. "I wonder what's taking them so long." She twitched her focus on the door, the window, me.

Carper took a sip of his tea. "I'm making you uncomfortable."

Alexis squirmed.

With eyes widened, I motioned for Carper to say something that'd break the awkward but obvious statement.

"Thank you for the bread, Alexis, but I prefer to eat outside. It's a nice view...well, if you like charred nature."

When Alexis didn't respond, Carper nodded his head. "I'll see both of you soon when we join the Lesaries." He turned and pursued the door.

"Wait." Alexis looked at Carper for the first time. "You'll be joining us then?"

"I have nowhere else to go." He glanced at me. "Nor anywhere else I'd rather be."

"Then you must stay with us." Alexis lifted her chin.

"Your grace means everything to me." He paused and tapped his fingers on the counter. "Well, then. I guess I'll be going."

"I'd rather you stay and take a seat."

Carper paused and looked to me. I shrugged my shoulders.

"Have my chair." I sat on the floor.

Carper sat and faced Alexis. "What's this all about?"

Alexis wet her lips. "I wasn't going to open the past, but since Pero's curious and it looks like I'll have a family with both of you, it's time for me to share. I might be able to get it all out before the Lesaries arrive."

Carper and I stayed silent as anticipation pumped into our veins.

"About eighteen years ago—"

My heart picked up speed.

"—I was at home. Sam had already left to live with his uncle on Earth, and a stranger came into the house. I didn't know who he was, had never seen him before. No one ever came out here. But he, uh…"

I closed my eyes, knowing where she was going with this, hoping to be wrong.

"He said he needed my help, that I'd be the perfect fit for a project."

I let out the breath I'd been holding, then adrenaline sent a wave of heat through me. Did I really want to know who my father was? He could've been a terrible man, for all I knew.

"A little over a year later, I had a baby girl." She folded her hands in her lap, thumbs twirling. "I agreed to the offer because of circumstances that I won't get into now. The moment my baby was born, my joy renewed." A smile spread. "I loved her very, very much. When Sam returned shortly after, he loved her." She gave a short laugh. "He taught her stories about Elohim and the Lesaries. Told her all kinds of sweet things. He used to call her, *my little chosen*."

My breath stalled, hands sweating. "Then what happened?"

"A woman came out of nowhere, claimed this place was hers. My baby started to cry, and I left to get her, but she disappeared. For years, I searched and prayed for an opening." Alexis stood and faced the fire.

She'd remembered Mom being at the tree, but not me, and she must've not recognized Mom when she came to the Lesaries' camp seventeen years later.

"I know where she is."

Alexis brought out a fresh loaf of bread to a small table. "Don't get my hopes up, Pero." She pulled out a knife and sliced a loaf that had cooled. "You don't know me, Dr. Carper."

"Please, call me Calvin."

Setting down her knife, she wiped a brow. "I was a surrogate mother for one of your experiments."

Carper cleared his throat. "You'll need to be more specific. I hate to admit I hired a lot of surrogates in the name of science."

"I'm pretty sure this was your biggest project, and it failed when your team could no longer find your subject."

Carper leaned forward. "The missing girl. She was yours?"

Alexis nodded, tears brimming. "Her name was Ruth."

Me. But what were they talking about? Was Alexis not my mother?

Carper placed an elbow on his knee and his forehead against his hand. He closed his eyes.

"Would someone mind explaining?"

Someone thumped two knocks on the door, then opened.

"Pero!" Shea's smile brought a sliver of sunshine to a room that matched the dire landscape around our safe haven. "Praise Elohim, you're alive!"

The news would need to wait. Our leader was here, and surely he'd guide us to greener pastures.

32

安全

Reunions are the best. Especially when they involved my parents. When I rushed into their open arms, Mom hugged me so tight I thought I might faint and Dad smothered my head with kisses.

They'd waited two years for my return. I couldn't fathom what not knowing must've done to them, but here they stood right in front of me, together, as if circumstances had never drifted them a part.

I wiped the tears from my face, scrunching my nose to hold back a sob. "I missed you so much."

Mom tucked me to her side. "You're safe, Pero. It's all over."

Those were the words that broke the wall of my dam, and they released as a flood that swept away all of the pain, the long-suffering, and, oh, the lifetime hunger to be free! But I no longer tasted freedom. I swallowed it, let it settle into my body and make itself at home.

Great, satisfying freedom. And no running shoes were needed to take me there.

Thank you, Elohim.

What wonders to be His child! To settle into the depth of His mercy and grace.

ONE WEEK later in the late afternoon, we were still walking. We moved forward until Elohim directed us to pause. Meanwhile, we searched along the horizon for a solution to the dead soil. No promise of a miracle, but Shea told us to keep believing. It was a slow and steady walk, not a race but definitely not a marathon. More like a stroll.

Mom had gone off to chat with her friends, including Cherry who was happily back together with Jehoshua. Cathena had appeared from Earth and joined us in our walk nearly an hour earlier. I spotted her not too far in front of me and Dad, her charismatic laughter enhancing her natural beauty. I had yet to talk with her. Something about the fact that she'd hung out with Henry without me was unsettling.

Dad nudged me, then toward Cathena. "Does it hurt?"

I shook my head to alert myself to the present. "A little. Henry and I weren't the right fit, but he was my best friend too. And I think not seeing my friend anymore is what hurts the most."

Dad nodded. "Makes sense. I'm proud of you, Pero. I don't know any other young ladies who could come out of what you did with a smile."

I laid my head against his shoulder. "Do you think it's over?"

"You bet."

"You seem confident."

"I am, because now when you go through something difficult in the future—and we all do in some way or another— you're going to know how to face it. You've grown resilient. Plus, your trust in Elohim has deepened, and that can only lead to victory no matter the outcome."

I squeezed him tight. "I love you, Pitar."

Dad chuckled. "Haven't heard you use that name in a while."

"Well, you better get used to it because I don't plan on going anywhere without you and Mom."

"Just wait a few years, and you might change your mind."

I pulled away. "Is it strange to be reunited with Mom?"

"Never. In many ways, it feels like she's always been here. Our love for each other is a forever covenant. Time can't make that different."

I sighed. "Do you think I'll find that kind of love someday?"

"Patience, sweetie. It will happen."

Carper ran from a distance and didn't stop till he was in front of me. He paused, holding onto his knees while panting. "Shea says we'll be setting up camp in the next hour."

I kept moving. "You rushed all the way here to tell us that?"

"No. Actually, I was hoping I could talk with you as we walk. You deserve an explanation."

"If you mean from when you and Alexis got all mysterious and didn't fill me in, then I agree."

"Sorry to give you angst. I needed time to process before sharing."

"I guess Alexis did too. She still hasn't talked with me either."

Carper placed his hands into his pockets. "I met with her a couple of days ago."

I swiveled to face him. "You told her she could be my birth mom?"

"No. I told her she needed to tell you everything, and I assumed you'd tell her who you are."

"Want some privacy?" Dad asked.

"Stay here," Carper said. "It will make my story easier to share."

I gulped. "You're making me nervous, Carper."

"Wish I could change that, but I'm nervous as hell. *Heck* is what I meant to say."

Clutching Dad's hand, I nodded for Carper to continue...er, start.

"Pero, I've done a lot of bad things in my life."

"I'm aware."

"Right." He cleared his throat. "There's one thing I did that was intended for my own selfish gain, but Elohim used it to be the greatest blessing I could've asked for."

Was he choking up?

"As the leader of Moon City, I always sought ways to discover new abilities, things that ordinary people could do if given the right ingredients, or what special people could do with those same ingredients. As much as I didn't want to admit it at the time, the Lesaries were special because they had power. Not as much as the three chosen or the transporters, but I wanted to try using them to create better potential in a human being than anyone had ever seen before. I hired women as surrogates, and their babies became the Warriors. Some of the Warriors came from their mothers' egg and I only needed to donate the sperm to create an embryo.

"When I sent out one of my workers to find a Lesarie woman, he came back and reported that he found someone who'd agreed to the arrangement. A woman named Alexis who lived alone. She said she'd only do it if the baby could be her own."

I tilted my head and bit my lip. "So, my mom is definitely Alexis."

"Yes, she is."

My heart beat faster. "I hoped it was her." Alexis was kind and considerate, everything I could wish for in a second mom. I imagined her face lighting up when I gave her the news. The whole situation felt strange, yet also just right. A perfect fit.

"That's a lot to take in," Dad said. "Did you know the sperm donor?"

Wait. Who was my father? Was he also kind? I'd been so focused on finding out about my birth mom, that I'd forgotten a man would be involved. *Duh, Pero. Of course, there's a man.*

I gave Dad a reassuring smile. "Whoever it is, you and Mom aren't being replaced. I'd never do that to you."

"It's okay, love." He kissed my head. "It's important for you to know about your birth parents. I'm right here with you."

When I looked back to Carper, he was no longer walking next to us but had moved to the side of the line of people and bent over, trembling underneath a tree. Dad and I met him, and I placed a hand on his arm.

"It's just me, Carper. I'm like a daughter to you, remember? You can tell me."

His face lifted, eyes brimming with tears. "I'm afraid I'll lose you, like I lost Cherry."

I shook my head. "You didn't lose her. Cherry needs time, that's all."

He wiped a tear, then averted his gaze and muttered. "It's me."

My hand dropped.

"What did you say?" Dad asked the question I couldn't mutter.

Carper couldn't have said what I thought he said. It had to be a mistake. There was no way that he—

"I was the donor." He cried hard, turning his head away.

I didn't move, couldn't speak. All these months singing songs together in prison, forgiving one another for our wrongs, cheering each other on when there was no one else but the fleas—this man who'd become like a second father to me was of my own blood.

No way.

Carper sniffled, then rubbed his face on his sleeve. "You don't need to say anything right now." He turned to Dad.

"Matthew, you don't know how sorry I am for stealing your family from you. She's always been your girl, and she's...you must be so proud."

Dad cleared his throat. "Thank you, Dr. Carper. That means a lot to me, but I have room in my heart for you to be proud of her also."

Carper cried harder.

Compassion overwhelmed me, building in my body like an ocean waiting to pour over another's wounded soul. I rushed into Carper's arms and cried with him.

"I forgive you," I said. "*Wǒ ài nǐ, Bàba.*"

He pulled back and gave some distance. "I love you too, *xīn gān bǎo bèi.*"

I scrunched my nose. "How come I don't look Chinese?"

Dad and Carper laughed.

"Genetics aren't always strong enough to produce clone-like children."

I grinned. "What about sarcasm?"

"Ha! I'm sorry to say you got that from me."

I cocked my head. "One more question."

"Anything."

"In the Forbidden City lab, you said you didn't find anything special about my blood."

"True."

"So, your experiment failed?"

Carper winked. "I'd say Elohim made you the greatest success in the history of all my experiments. Do you agree, Matthew?"

"You bet."

With a wide smile, I took a hold of Dad's hand, and with my other, held onto Carper's.

Two men—distinct yet strong—so dear to my heart.

WE'D HAD our fill of soup and bread. A crew cleaned up the mess, and Alexis rested her feet against a log and reached her hands for the warmth of the fire. Tents had been set up, ready for the night. I'd gotten used to sleeping on bamboo, cots, the ground. I didn't mind so much, and there was always a line of people waiting for Cherry's Chinese massage the next morning. Apparently, she'd gone to school to learn how to pop joints and loosen knots.

I sat near Alexis. Mom and Dad had given us space. We were finally to have the conversation I'd been anxious to finish.

Alexis told me the rest of the story, the same one Carper had said. It was harder to hear from Alexis' perspective. Carper had been the perpetuator of the scenario, while Alexis had taken the opportunity out of a life-long dream of having a baby. She hadn't ever met someone to share life with and marry and figured that being in her early forties, it was too late to see her prayers answered. But shortly after she had her baby, she lost me. At least Sam returned to her. Yet for years she'd mourned over me having gone missing. I didn't know clearly why Elohim allowed it, but He had, and Sam and I had made a mom-swap.

After she shared, we stopped to listen to the crackling fire, the Lesaries' conversations and music that some danced to in the background.

I took a big breath, readying myself for what I knew Alexis didn't. I was her missing daughter, and she my mother. The woman who birthed me, held me, shared her lullabies.

"You still sing to her, don't you?"

Alexis brought her legs down from the log. "Want me to get you more soup? There's a little left."

"Alexis." I waited till she met my eyes. "I don't want to talk about food."

In the summer when I first met her, Alexis cared for me with a meal, bath, a place to rest. Just as a mother would do. But she didn't know she was my mother then, nor did she appear to recognize it now. We both had the gift of music and perhaps the same desire to retreat or divert the conversation when things were tough.

But if words didn't speak to her, I'd give her a song.

"Do not worry about tomorrow. Don't you worry about today."

Alexis peered up. "It's your voice." She put a hand over her trembling lips. "I've heard your voice in my dreams for months. Elohim told me to sing back. I didn't understand why."

I stood and took a step forward, my own voice becoming as unsteady as my footing. "I know why. It's because I needed to find you. My name is Pero Ruth Moshe. Seventeen years old. Adopted daughter of a woman who found me one day under a tree in the forest, and when she picked me up, disappeared with me into another universe."

Alexis clenched her fists, knuckles turning white.

"That same woman, Bahar, married a man who also adopted me and raised me when she disappeared again. I was left alone without my mother just as Sam was left alone without his father. Sam found his birth mom, Bahar. And I found my birth mom, Alexis."

Alexis studied my face, unable to speak.

"It could be Elohim allowed me to disappear from you that day so that I could grow up to be Sam's chosen, just as the prophecy said would happen. Then again, Sam is gone, so I'm unsure if Elohim will direct us to be together or not. But I do know that Elohim brought me to Origo, not only to rescue Bahar, save Dr. Carper, and unlock the sanctuary in Beijing. I was also brought back to Origo for you. I am your Ruth."

Alexis burst into tears, and just like the picture of the child who once laid on an altar—forsaken and abandoned—I was brought into the safety of my mother's arms.

EPILOGUE
FIVE YEARS LATER

We are nomads. As we travel, Elohim provides meals from clouds that rain bread and rocks that, when cracked with Shea's staff, shoot out water. Our once green world still lives in sepia tone. Nothing that we plant lives. Rain never relieves us. Even the sun's power has dimmed, as if Origo has aged beyond her golden years. The only remaining beauty in all of creation is the setting and rising sun. Evolving colors of pink, red, and orange remind me that in the midst of suffering, Elohim's beauty still displays.

Of course, the Lesaries are the brightest and most beautiful creation. Our group has expanded to tens of thousands, and we keep growing while sharing the same heart and passion to love Elohim and walk where He leads. We come from different worlds, represent a variety of ethnicities and languages. When we arrived in Origo, Elohim gave us the gift of speaking the same language so we could all understand each other, yet the variety of skin pigmentation, hair color, and ages make us the best-looking sunset I've ever seen.

No longer do I run. There is no need. I live a simple life of dependance on Him. Not the kind I had with Henry. I've grown from that, have learned it's best to make my own decisions and not use others as a crutch out of fear that I'll be left behind or run too far. Now, I lean on a greater power that's more magnificent than a chosen's feather or a transporter's leap to another world.

The Lesaries have become powerful, but not because we have a building like Carper thought he'd be king of; not because we hid underground from our persecutors; and not because we broke a wall. Our power comes from a single cloud that hovers over our heads. It's a bright cloud, a cloud of presence that brings us courage and hope, perseverance and faith.

Elohim is power.

I never feel out of place here. Never question whether this is where I should be. Elohim's brought me family. He's built a kingdom among us.

"Elohim's kingdom isn't about the talk," Shea once said. "It's about Elohim's power."

"So, *we* are the kingdom."

Shea spread his arm wide, displaying the mass of people trudging through a dead land. "And aren't we a masterpiece?"

Yes, we are.

Alexis' dream of marriage and having a child came true. A year after Carper and I landed in the older universe, Shea and Alexis were married. Along with Jehoshua and Cherry, they're the best leaders I could ask for. I've slowly started calling Alexis *mom*, but it's easy to mix up both my moms when we're together, so most of the time, Alexis remains Alexis.

I call Carper my Chinese dad, and he calls me his Chinese daughter. Cherry and Carper's relationship improves every day. They are comfortable with each other, and I've even seen them exchanging hugs now and then.

Dad's still my number one fan. Since he's been following

Elohim, his anxiety has reduced, and his days are full of joy instead of fear.

Dad and Mom love each other more than I imagined after being separated for so long and live the kind of relationship I still dream of at twenty-two. Me at seventeen feels so long ago. It was the year my life changed completely.

Henry still appears in my dreams occasionally, but more distant now, coming to good endings but becoming shorter each night. I can't deny I still miss him. Cathena still lives here. At times it feels awkward when she talks about Henry in the way I used to, but I now consider Cathena my best friend. Although the bond and love Henry and I had was real, I can't say that Henry was mine the way Dad and Mom are for each other. As much as Henry loved me, I wouldn't go as deep to say that I was his chosen.

Lately, I can't get Sam out of my mind.

Once a month, Faith flies two letters from Sam, addressed to Alexis and Mom. I never understood how the letters travel from one universe to the next, but there are many things Elohim's done that I can't fathom in my little, finite mind.

By this time, Sam's heard about me being Alexis' and Carper's birth daughter, and I sometimes wonder if the news makes Sam love me more, now that it's certain we're not related and that I am the Ruth he loved from the start. Alexis shares the letters with me when she's done reading. I don't know if she would if Sam didn't end each letter with a *P.S. Say hi to my Ruth*. There's never any indicator that he expects us to marry just because of a prophecy. In some ways, I think he recognizes the need for healing from past pain just as much as I do for myself. But I am healing, slowly, and at times I wonder if he has too and if he's thought of me beyond being his Ruth.

In the letters, Sam shared that Green Meadow's also no longer green and is slowly turning the same black that we've grown accustomed to seeing. Yet Sam feels he's supposed to stay. So many already have left Green Meadow, and the once small town has become even smaller. Lately, Carper has thought about moving to Green Meadow to be "king" of the small sanctuary building I drove by so many times on my way to and from school, the Lesaries who'd talked about wanting a king for so long. I told him if he goes, I'm coming along too.

Sam never mentions another woman. He's now roughly a year or two older than me because he wouldn't age as quickly on Earth. It seems he would've met someone by now. In my dreams the last few weeks, Sam's digging a shovel into the soil, but the dirt stays rock hard. The dreams are the same every night. After Sam works on plowing the soil with no success, I appear in the field with my feather pendent. As I sing Elohim's lullaby, the dirt becomes soft so Sam can work once more.

Last night's dream was different. Instead of singing the lullaby, I sang the song I wrote for Mom years ago.

"I'm running after you. Won't let anything in my way. I'm running after you. Coming home, coming home, coming home."

Sam looked up from the soil, shovel in his hand and sweat on his brow.

"Ruth," he said, "my pretty chosen one. Come home."

I woke up with the image of his deep brown eyes. They were like flashlights, imploring my soul, guiding the way. They were like doors, open and ready for me to fall into. If I go after him, I'm afraid I'll fall. Still scared, I guess, of tumbling into darkness with no way out. Like Carper and I did when landing in Mr. Rose's mansion and like Henry and I did from the pot to under the Forbidden City.

But Elohim walked with me in those frightening places, and maybe the darkness as well as the light is a part of His plan. Sometimes things must die before the world sees the life they can bring.

Day after day, Elohim speaks the same words to me, like an echoing song as vivid as last night's dream.

Follow the light.
Follow the song.
Follow the King.

No need to fear. In fact, maybe I'll take another leap of faith and answer Sam's invitation to come home. After all, a fall doesn't last forever.

AUTHOR'S NOTE

"China so filled my heart and mind that there was no rest."

— J. HUDSON TAYLOR

Nineteen-year-old me on the Great Wall in Beijing

The other day, I ran into an old friend who said he still dreams about China. I understood what he meant. Some experiences in life have us wishing for a travel machine (maybe one that looks like a cement mixer) that would let us relive the excitement of an adventure.

In 2002, I first joined a team from the Pacific Northwest and taught cultural lessons to high school students for their summer camp. We traveled to Kunming, Shanghai, Beijing, and Hong Kong. I ended up teaching in

China for four summers and even met my then future husband, who was on the same team for several of those trips.

The first time I visited the Forbidden City in Beijing, I said to myself, "If I ever write a novel, I want it to be set here." I found such mystery in the vast, historical landmark and beauty in the gardens and people. While *Forbidden Reign* is fiction, all of the locations in the novel are inspired by actual places I visited.

Like Henry and Pero, my friends (not me) climbed into a large pot in The Palace Museum, and many of the locals asked if we were celebrities. I *did* eat chicken feet, which isn't that bad. Does that make me a hero?

China will always fill my heart and mind. I'm grateful to relive my perspective of this incredible country's culture through one of my favorite ways to share anything.

A story.

ACKNOWLEDGMENTS

Wow! How did I get here again?

Jesus, you are my hero. Thank you for giving me a global church to do life with.

Eric Earls, thank you for your continual love and support and for watching the girls when I send myself to my room.

Haven and Sadie, thanks for letting Mom write and dreaming with me. Hugs and kisses.

Elisha, my precious Chinese girl, Aunt Amy loves you.

To my critique group and dear friends who've helped me tremendously with advice, edits, and cheers: Karen Grunst, Karen Barnett, Christina Nelson, Heidi Gaul, Don White. You are the greatest author community I could hope for.

Readers and fans, thank you for your virtual letter responses. Your encouragement keeps me going forward. On werto and koach to you.

ABOUT THE AUTHOR

Best-selling author **Amy Earls** writes fiction that explores intersections between life issues and faith. A professor of first-year college students, she holds a master's degree in education for adult learners, with an emphasis on writing. Amy lives in Oregon's Willamette Valley with her husband, daughters, and a never-dying goldfish.

Learn more about Amy, her virtual letters, and free offers at www.AmyEarls.com.

MORE BY AMY EARLS

Want to know if Pero answers Sam's call? Go to amyearls.com/meadowscurse or scan the QR code below to find out now!